A
Virgin
At Fifty

Jack S. Mill

Jack S. Miller

Blurb Edition

©2020, all rights reserved.

Cover by: Coby Blaze™ Designs

License Notes

Introduction

Finally after 50 years, Ben didn't have to fly his eyeballs over a woman's dress trying to have a glimpse of what it looks like. Never in his thoughts had he ever imagined a beautiful woman like Christine not even Sophia would show their undies until that day...

Synopsis

They showed men and women doing it in all sorts of positions, and he probably was teaching Sophia some of these kinky things. Ben wanted to fuck, he didn't want to have to beat off like this.

He felt ashamed and disgusted with himself. Just a few days ago, he had all the ass that he could handle: Sophia of course, and then there had been Christine and Mercy. But now, he had only his fist to give him relief. Sophia was into men. He'd seen her downtown a couple of times with some real old guys, guys with grey hair and all-that was when she wasn't running around with that horny Scoutmaster. Ben wished that Christine had stayed in-town, over at Aunt Sophia's.

Chapter 1

... Pussy just like that. Actually, until this moment, Ben, who was fifteen years old, had never seen a cunt in the flesh before.

"Listen-if you wanted to see my snatch, why didn't you just ask, instead of dislocating your eyeballs trying to catch a flash?" Christine said and opened her knees wider so that her fat, hairy cunt lips gaped, and the moist, pink slices of inner flesh showed.

"Haven't you ever seen a twat before?"

Ben blinked. His cock had grown so stiff that it hurt. Good grief! He could see everything, even her asshole, pink and puckered. His prick swelled until he thought it would burst out of his Boy Scout uniform shorts. With embarrassment, he saw Christine was looking right at the wet spot where the tip of his rock-hard rod showed under the khaki cloth. He tried to look away from what she was showing him, but the gaping girl-crack drew his eyes like a magnet.

"I guess you haven't," Christine said.

"W-w-w-hat?" Ben stammered. "Haven't what?" His throat was dry and his heart hammered in his chest. Did she want him to fuck her?

"Come over here, Benie," Christine said slowly.

Ben couldn't straighten up. His prick throbbed under his tightly stretched Boy Scout shorts as he bent forward and hopped over to the couch where his girl cousin was calmly spreading her cunt lips for him.

"Might as well get a good close look, if this is your first time, Benie. Here, sit on the floor. You can get your face up close. It won't bite you." Christine slid her ass forward so that her quim was right under Ben's nose.

He squatted before his cousin, his eyes level with the top of her glistening slit. He could smell a strange, wild, clean, but definitely girl odor. Mygosh! He was smelling a girl's cunt!

Christine squeezed a triangular piece of naked pink flesh at the top of her hairy crack, and a pink pearl of meat glistened.

"That's my clit, Benie," Cousin Christine explained. "That's what makes a girl feel-oh, so good, umm." She teased the pink, pea-sized nub of flesh with her slim finger. "Wanna fuck me, Benie?"

Ben thought his pants would explode. The tip of his steel-hard prick peeked out from the bottom of his shorts, dribbling a pearl of thin but sticky juice. "Uh, sure, Christine, I'm game."

"Then take your pants down and lets see what you got," the girl said and reached for the painfully hard ridge in his pants. The touch of her fingers on his dick, even through the thin material of uniform and undershorts, made his rod lengthen another inch. "Hurry up," the girl said as he fumbled with his pants. She was fingering her clit with rapid strokes.

Ben watched her with wonder. So that's what girls did instead of jerking off! He unzipped his pants, and pulled them down along with his undershorts. His prick sprang out, an angry purple rod of meat that the girl grasped with her free hand and squeezed lightly. Ben reached for his girl cousin's spread-open cunt, but hesitated.

"Put your fingers into me," Christine said. Her voice was hoarse and her face flushed.

"Come on, touch me." There was a wild look in her eyes and her blonde hair fell over her face as she pulled Ben towards her by his prick. He put his fingers between her open thighs and ran their tips along the rim of her slimy crack. The thought of shoving his aching cock into her so excited him that he nearly spilled his load. How would it feel to slip his prick in between those wet, pink lips, into the girl's eagerly waiting cunt-hole?

Christine stopped flicking her clit and grabbed his head by the hair and kissed him giving him tongue so that he could feel it all the way down to his cock. He kissed her back and down there felt her guiding his rock-hard prick into her warm, wet snatch.

Christine rolled back on the couch, pulling him on top^ of her. His prick stayed lodged in her as he found himself lying between smooth-skinned, soft girl-thighs, his balls pressed against the crack of his cousin's ass, and his prick stuck up her cunt. He rammed his cock in as far as it would go and heard Christine wince.

"Wow, you're big, Benie," she said and started moving her hips under him.

Ben pulled back and thrust forward again, feeling his prick slide way up inside of her. He was fucking! He was finally getting his first piece of ass! And what an ass! Wait until he told the fellows in the Scout troop about it!

"C'mon," Christine urged, "give it to me, Benie." Her hips ground away under him, and

Ben felt his prick rubbing the length of his cousin's cunt sheath as he laid his strokes into her, feeling his balls slap against her spread-open asshole.

"Christine! Benie!" The voice cut through Ben's pleasure, and he stopped in mid-stroke.

Oh no, not now, not when he was about to finish his first piece of ass!

"Never mind her," Christine said and bucked her belly and cunt against him, "You just keep fucking, Benie."

"Where are you two?" Aunt Sophia's voice was strident, chilling. Ben felt his prick go soft. He couldn't let Sophia catch him screwing Christine.

"What's the matter with you?" Christine said, her breath short and hard. "Keep on fucking."

"Aunt Sophia," Ben said as his prick as soft as an overdone spaghetti noodle shrank and slipped out of the girl's cunt.

"Hell, who cares about her?" Christine said, pulling him back down on top of her.

"I can't," Ben said. "I just can't with her about to bust in here any moment." He slipped into his pants, kicking the undershorts beneath the couch. Christine shrugged, sat up, and pulled her dress down barely in time.

"What are you two doing in here?" Sophia asked as she came clacking into the room. She was a tall, full-bodied woman of twenty-nine, with fair skin and dark hair.

Her green eyes took in her niece's spread thighs and flushed cheeks and then came to rest on Ben. He crossed his legs to hide the wet spot on his uniform shorts and tried to avoid Aunt Sophia's eyes. He stole a look at her legs though and at her large, powerful ass, when she swung around and turned to Christine.

"Well, young lady?" Sophia asked. "What's been going on in here?" She sniffed and frowned. "What's that smell, Christine?"

The girl brushed her blonde hair back from her face and gave her aunt a teasing look, a smirk on her dark pink lips. "Don't you know, Auntie?" she said and slid forward on the couch so that her dress rode up and her aunt as well as Ben could see her bare, hairy snatch.

Ben's balls ached. He looked at Aunt Sophia's ass and imagined what it would be like to pull it apart and thrust his eight inches of steel-hard gristle into his aunt's cunt. It would probably be tight, he thought, and the idea of making her take in his full eight inches of cock, with her squirming and hollering, excited him and made his balls hurt even more.

"You should be ashamed of yourself!" Sophia said to her niece. "Showing yourself to a boy like that! And one with a dirty mind like Benie to boot! Don't you know what it does to a boy when you expose your private parts to him like that?"

"It makes him get a hard-on," the blonde girl said and ran her pink tongue over her lips.

"Well of all the-!" Sophia raised her hand as if to slap Christine, then let it drop. "I'll deal with you later, young lady." She turned to Ben. Her tits jiggled in her black dress as she reached for his ear and took it between two fingers. She pulled Ben to his feet and he saw Christine titter as he unsuccessfully tried to cover the spot on his pants.

"You filthy little beast!" Sophia shrilled at her nephew. "You became so excited at seeing your cousin's--your own cousin's-private parts that you soiled your pants!" Sophia turned back to Christine. "You see what you did to your cousin, Christine?" she said. "Some day you'll do that to a boy and he'll lose control and then where will you be, young lady?"

"On my back with a man's meat up my-"

"That'll do!" Sophia cut off her niece. "Go to your room-at once!

Christine got up, slowly, and walked out, swinging her ass. Benie watched it and her slim girl-legs.

Gosh! I fucked her, Ben thought. I had that ass naked under me and those smooth, tanned legs wrapped around my waist, and my cock way up her cunt-hole, sliding in and out-gosh it felt good, all squishy and warm. I fucked a girl! He was full of wonder at how easy it had been after wishing for it and thinking about it for such a long time.

But I didn't finish, Benie thought. I wanted to fill that hot-assed little bitch's belly full of my cum! Ben's balls ached so badly, he was feeling sick.

"All right, you filthy little brute!" Sophia said and pulled Ben by his ear. "You march right upstairs, young man. I have a bone to pick with you."

Ben felt the pain in his ear as his aunt marched him toward the stairwell. What could she be so put out about now? As she forced him to go up the stairs, doubled over,

Ben could see his aunt's thighs and belly under her black dress, and if he strained against her pinched fingers on his ear, lie could glimpse her full tits. He felt his prick getting stiff again as the thought came to him that he would like to get his nuts off inside of that woman, his aunt Sophia. After all, she did have all the equipment, tits, ass, and a cunt, probably with a big black bush around it.

"Now!" Sophia said and let go of Ben's ear. As he straightened, he saw her holding up his magazines with the brightly colored photographs-his ."Fuck books" as he called them.

"This, this horrible filth, Benie, where on earth did you get this trash?" She was holding the magazines as if they were full of spunk and cunt juice. "And hiding it under your mattress, like a thief! No wonder you have bad thoughts and get all excited when your cousin Christine is careless about her skirt!"

"They're mine," Ben said reaching for the magazines. "You leave 'em alone."

"I certainly will do no such thing," Sophia said. "I'm confiscating them, and don't you ever let me catch you with anything like that again or I'll report you to your Scoutmaster."

Ben wanted to blurt out that he had swiped the magazines from his Scoutmaster's backpack during the Scout troop's last camp trip, but he decided to keep his mouth shut.

Sophia narrowed her green eyes and put her pretty face right near Ben's freckled boy's features. "If you weren't so big-" she said. "Even so, I've a good mind to take your pants down and give you a good licking-on the bare."

The idea of lying bare from the waist down across his aunt's lap made Ben's cock stiffen some more. Now if Aunt Sophia's lap happened to be bare-the thought of his stiff prick probing between her thighs brought back a full hard-on.

"Now, you just stay up here in your room, young man," Sophia said, "and don't you think I won't tell your parents about this? She held up the magazines and sailed out. Ben sat down on the bed, his cock throbbing in his shorts. He opened his fly and let it spring out. He stroked its sticky length and then sniffed his fingers. They smelled of her, Christine, of her cunt.

I've got to finish banging her, Ben thought, as he stroked his prick, faster and faster.

I don't want to jerk off like some little boy, not now, not after I've tasted the real thing.

Walking as quietly as he could, he went out the door and looked up and down the upstairs hall. There was no sign of Aunt Sophia. Ben snuck towards the stairs, tiptoed past Aunt Sophia's room, wincing when a floorboard creaked, and then stopped when he heard a moan coming from behind the white door. Was she sick? But no, there it was again, a long, drawn out sigh breaking into a whimper. There was nothing sick about that sound. It was like the little groans Christine was beginning to make when he had been fucking her, just before Sophia had interrupted them.

Ben bent down and peeked through the keyhole. At first, he saw only the bed with its white crochet spread. He had to look in at an angle to see something more than that. He could not believe his eyes! There, upright on the dresser, leaning against the mirror, was one of his "fuck books," a magazine, swiped from the Scoutmaster, that showed couples fucking and sucking. The book was open to a color photograph, a close-up of an angry-red, veined prick spitting thick, white cum. If he pressed his cheek against the door he could see a luscious pair of female legs, the black skirt up high, exposing smooth, white thighs. Ben squeezed his head against the wood as hard as he could until he could see what Sophia was doing. Her hand was between her thighs, jerking rapidly up and down as if she were strumming a guitar, and all the time, from her half-open mouth she let out these little whimpers and moans. Ben's cock throbbed with longing, when he realized what Sophia was up to. She-was diddling herself! She was looking at a full-color photo of a man's prick squirting spunk and strumming her clit. Then Ben saw that it wasn't just the photo of a prick that Sophia was using to get herself hot. Right next to it there stood propped against the dresser mirror the picture of this TV guy Ben remembered her watching. She must be imagining that it was his prick that was creaming and way up inside of her cunt!

Sophia was gasping and squirming, her bare ass grinding against the seat of her chair, her black hair over her flushed face, eyes closed, as she lifted both bare feet off the carpet and put them up on the dresser top. Ben's cock was so hard, it hurt.

He could not believe this! Before today he had never seen a naked cunt before, and here in less than an hour, he had not only been shown a girl's quim and had fucked for the first time, but now was seeing a woman, a beautiful woman nearly twice his age, about to get herself off.

Sophia had spread her legs so wide that Ben could see the coral pink slit in her black bush, above fat, pale ass-cheeks, reflected in the mirror. She seemed to be having trouble getting herself satisfied, because her head was thrown back and her lips were open, revealing her white, even teeth, as she puffed and strained. Ben shook his head as he remembered the prim and proper Sophia that had received him only last night. She had told him that she hoped he was as clean in mind as a Scout should be. She had reprimanded his cousin Christine for sitting carelessly, although the blonde girl had been wearing panties that time. Sophia had lectured him on the importance of a cold bath before going to bed for a growing boy and on the merits of tennis and other exhausting sports to keep his mind filled with wholesome thoughts. Now, this same twenty-nine-year-old aunt was stripping down in her bedroom, while thinking about some TV actor's spunking cock. That was what Sophia was doing. She pulled the black dress up over her head, exposing her naked ass, fat, round cheeks that trembled as she impatiently flung the dress on the bed. What an ass! A real woman's ass, full and plump and made for squirming under a male while he fucked her good and hard as she needed to be reamed.

Sophia unhooked her brassiere and for the first time, Ben saw her full-fleshed tits in the raw. The nipples were a dusky rose as she fingered them to make them stiff, and she felt herself up, squeezing her boobs, grinding her thighs together, moaning for a cock. Ben stroked his own as he watched his aunt finger-fucking herself, opening her snatch wide, showing the wet, dark-red inner skin, thrusting two, three, four fingers up into herself and ringing her snatch. But as Ben stroked his aching prick, his aunt still could not get the relief she wanted and needed. She opened her dresser drawer and took out a thick, white candle. Ben had heard that women fucked themselves with candles, but he never had believed it-until now. Here, his aunt was about to shove a wax candle up her burning quim. As Ben beat his meat, he wondered if both their problems would not be solved were he to knock on the door and offer to shove his aching rock-hard rod up his aunt's red-hot quim. The thought nearly made him spill his spunk. But he kept it in, watching in wonder as his aunt dipped her fingers into a jar of Vaseline and greased up the hefty candle before bending her knees, spreading her cunt lips and starting to ride up and down on the wax rod. As she candle-fucked herself, she turned in circles, so that Ben could see her trembling ass-cheeks one second, and her heavy boobs and hungry cunt, sucking on the candle there as if it were a coral-lipped mouth, up and down, up and down, the next.

Suddenly Ben felt a hand grab his cock, a soft, female hand, and he could smell Christine's scent just before she pulled him down on top of herself, her shift up above her tits, her long, blonde hair spread like a halo on the hall rug as she guided his prick up into her cunt. This time she was writhing under him before he had finished his first fuck stroke. He never knew anything could feel as good as this! The soft girl-flesh was drawing his spunk from him, the tight rim of Christine's cunt moving up and down on his nine inches-it felt as big to Ben-of hard man meat. He could feel Christine's ass rolling under him, a naked girl-ass, and Ben grabbed the cheeks and felt his fingertips in the crack of his pretty cousin's ass, the middle fingers digging into her velvet-soft bung-hole. Christine moaned as he fingered her asshole, while he drove his nine inches of cock way up into her belly. Then he heard himself shouting and he bucked his ass up high before driving his cock into his cousin's cunt faster and faster, like a piston, pressing her nakedness against the carpet, feeling his nuts explode as the first jet of hot spunk shot up into his sixteen-year-old cousin Christine's belly. He squirted spurt after spurt of cum, rubbing his cock up and down inside

Christine's cunt-sheath, forcing her up against his belly by squeezing her ass-cheeks, pulling them apart, until the last drop of his sticky, white juice had been squeezed out of him by his almost naked girl cousin.

Ben collapsed on top of the shuddering girl and lay there for what seemed ages. But it was actually less than a minute, and then Christine reached for Ben's semi-hard cock and started handling it. She closed her soft hand over the stiffening prick and started rubbing it up and down, the length of gristle still wet with cum and cunt juice.

The blonde teenager really knew how to give a hand job. Her ringers applied just the right amount of pressure, squeezing the male meat gently, running soft fingertips over the swelling tip, ringing the shaft, while she pressed her slim, naked girl-body against him. Ben reached for her tits and started feeling her up. He had never felt a girl's naked boobs before and as Christine's nipples became hard under his hand, his prick kept on swelling, urged on by Christine's hands that were both working his rod now.

Christine kissed her younger cousin full on the mouth, her hands both on his throbbing cock. She thrust her tongue into his mouth until his prick started to leak. Ben ran his hand over his girl cousin's naked ass, feeling the tender cheeks, squeezing the full flesh, and fingering her crack. He ran his hand under until he felt her wet cunt, but the girl twisted away from his probing hand and dropped his cock.

Ben looked up in surprise. He still could not understand girls. Why did she stroke him to a good stiff hard-on and then keep him from her cunt? But Christine surprised him again. She knelt, her bare ass high, and went for his cock with her mouth. She raised it, holding it with her lips, then propping it up with both hands, started to give him head. She inhaled his male gristle, and sucked on it, running her soft mouth up and down its entire length, tonguing it as she went, swallowing the drops of clear, sticky juice she drew out of it. Ben had never dared to dream of a girl sucking him off like that, and here was his older girl cousin, this good-looking blonde chick Christine going down on him, working him up so that he could fuck her again.

While Christine kept blowing him, Ben cupped her tits, feeling her stiff nipples, rolling them between his fingers, and then ran his palms over her bare back, leaning forward until he was at her up tilted, naked ass again, feeling up her taut ass-cheeks, the crack between them wide open. Ben fondled his cousin Christine's satin-soft bunghole and then let his fingertips slide down into the hot, wet slit of her quim. Christine thrust her ass up against his hand, so that his fingers slid way up inside of her.

Her soft, warm girl-mouth was working on Ben's prick, her tongue darting around his stiff meat, licking up every drop of cum that oozed from his throbbing dick. Then Christine scrambled around on her knees, her mouth rotating on the swollen shaft of Ben's cock, until her upraised, naked ass faced him, her gaping asshole and cunt inches from his face. Ben smelled the slightly sweaty fragrance of her quim and bung and looked with wonder at the wanton display of her femaleness. Fringed by a pubic beard of dark-blonde pussy hair, Christine's cunt lips were coral-pink, swollen and inflamed with lust. She was all animal, presenting her hot twat for the male's inspection, while she readied his meat for plunging into her swollen and gaping crack by sucking it for him with her mouth.

Ben saw the dark-rose clam of Christine's cunt, the puckered, pink ring of her asshole above it, framed by the fattish, velvety cheeks of her girlish ass. Peach fuzz of blonde hairs covered the inner curves of her buttocks, the golden down becoming thicker near the female body-holes.

Ben felt Christine's mouth draw up and off his prick. "Eat it," she said.

"W-w-wha-a-t?" Ben quavered.

"Lick it, suck it, Benie. Put your mouth to my snatch and work me up," his girl cousin commanded.

Benie gulped. He did not know whether he could lick that smelly, wet girl-meat. Christine thrust her ass back, and her drooling quim pressed against Ben's nose and mouth. Down by his prick, the teenage girl's mouth was doing things, to him that Ben had never imagined a girl would do to a boy. With the soft inner pads of her lips, Christine nibbled the underside of her cousin's cock, slightly back from the tip, where the nerves were most sensitive.

Ben's mouth watered suddenly at the thought of licking the tender girl-flesh that smelled slightly fishy, like fresh oysters. When he stuck his tongue out and in between the hot lips of his girl cousin's cunt, he tasted her salty quim juice. Kissing her there, on her wide-open cunt, was not much different from kissing a girl's mouth. Only the lips were fleshier, fatter down there, and the cunt smelled pungent, wild. As he ran his stiff tongue around the rim of the girl's snatch, Ben felt her spread her ass-cheeks even wider. The hot, wet girl cunt was glued to his face, and he started to suck her cunt-flesh. Ben swallowed her salty quim juice. He still could not believe that this was happening to him, Ben! Good Gosh, he was lapping a girl's cunt! Eating pussy, hair pie-muff-diving! Now he knew why they called it that. He had to come up for air from time to time, pull his nose out from between his cousin Christine's swollen cunt lips to fill his lungs before plunging back in again to eat the girl's meat.

Then he felt Christine's snatch contract, and she pulled her cunt and ass off his face and, as nimble and slender as an eel, twisted about, one bare foot thudding against Aunt

Sophia's bedroom door. Christine lay on her back, spread wide for him and pulled his purplish-red prick up into her cunt.

"Start fucking, Benie! Faster!" Christine urged. She bucked her belly up against him, and Ben fucked her, moving his hips up and down, as quickly as he could, rubbing his hard prick against the sheath of her cunt. The girl was grinding her bare ass against the carpet, keeping his prick inside of her, loving the fucking he was giving her, until he felt the first jet of spunk shoot into her belly, then the second, and another, and at that moment, Sophia opened her bedroom door and looked down at her niece and nephew writhing on the floor of her upstairs hallway.

"What on earth!" Sophia shrieked. "Oh, you dirty, filthy-" She reached for Ben's ear and pulled him off his cousin Christine. Ben saw that his aunt had put on a long, wine-colored robe, that was open to above her knees so that he could see her bare thighs. Grabbing Christine by her blonde hair, Sophia dragged both teenagers into her bedroom and turned the key, locking the door. She put the key into the pocket of her robe and took hold of Ben's ear once more.

Holding the nearly naked boy and girl-one by the ear, the other by her long, blonde hair-Sophia dragged them over to her bed. Ben was amazed at the strength of the woman as she flung him and Christine about as if they were dolls. Aunt Sophia's face was white with fury. Her nostrils flared and her red lips were drawn into a narrow slit.

She looked like a madwoman-, a possessed creature, and Ben was actually afraid of her. When she ordered him to kneel by the side of the bed, he did so, without protest, feeling awfully foolish in only his Boy Scout uniform shirt, his ass bare, and his prick and balls hanging out for his aunt to see.

But Sophia was not interested in his male equipment, she was giving her full attention to her blonde niece Christine. "You little slut," Sophia said through clenched teeth, as she sat down on the edge of the bed, on the white crochet bedspread, and yanked her teenage niece across her lap-the girl's naked ass uppermost.

Aunt Sophia's robe fell back from her bare legs, and Ben noticed the contrast of the teenage girl's suntanned body against the woman's ivory skin. But the portion of Christine's body that Sophia concentrated on was not tan but a golden cream color where a bikini bottom had covered her ass-cheeks. Aunt Sophia's palm smacked against the blonde teenage girl's naked ass with such fury that Ben winced.

"Slut!" Sophia raged. "I give you a place to stay when nobody else would, and this is how you repay me!"

Smack! The woman's palm came down on the girl's naked bottom again.

"You show up out of the blue, beg me to put you up, promise to behave, and the first chance you get, you do a filthy, nasty thing!"

Smack! Aunt Sophia's hand slapped the girl's quivering ass-cheeks.

"Incorrigible,"

Smack!

"That's what you are!"

Smack!

"If they'd given you a good licking in that reform school,"

Smack!

"Instead of letting you run away,"

Smack!

"You would have thought twice before doing a nasty, filthy thing like that with your cousin!"

Smack! Smack! Smack! Sophia spanked the seventeen-year-old girl's naked behind again and again.

Ben, kneeling half-naked, couldn't help feeling a pang in his prick, as he saw the girl kicking her long, bare legs, exposing the slit of her pussy, the cunt-hair flecked with a white speck of his spunk. Had he actually fucked this good-looking girl, now writhing across his aunt's lap? He still could not believe that he had actually had his prick up inside of this pretty, blonde girl whose ass was all red from the spanking she was getting.

But although it must have stung her, Christine did not seem to be in any great pain. She was shrieking, yes, but that was only to make her aunt think the spanking was doing more damage than it actually was. But Ben noticed that the squirming girl was getting Sophia all flustered. Before every smack, Christine raised her naked ass, letting the taut cheeks spread open, so that her aunt got a good view of her quim. Once or twice, Aunt Sophia's palm struck right across her niece's wide-open crack, and

Ben could have sworn that she let her hand linger on the girl's hairy cleft just for a fraction of a second longer than necessary, before administering the next spank. Sophia was flushed now, whether from the exertion of giving her niece a good spanking or from touching the girl's cunt lips, Ben could not tell. But it must have been the contact of her hand on the girl's exposed snatch, because, Sophia stopped hitting Christine for a second, reached down to yank off her slipper, and brought the sole of that down three times-each with an earsplitting crack-on the girl's bun.

This time red welts rose on Christine's ass and she cried out in real pain.

"That will teach you, young lady!" Sophia said and stood up so suddenly that Christine nearly fell to the floor. But Sophia caught her, and Ben noticed with astonishment that Sophia was cupping Christine's right boob as she helped the girl to her feet. There were tears on Christine's face, but they must have been a sham, because Christine gave

Ben a sly wink, when Sophia was adjusting her wine-colored robe.

"Get down there next to Benie, so you can see what he's going to get," Sophia said and reached for Ben's inflamed, red ear again. Christine squatted on her heels, knees apart, showing off her pink cunt-crack in its nest of dark-blonde hair. Sophia appeared not to notice as she flung her nephew across her lap, face down.

Ben felt a funny pang in his lower belly as his aunt's thighs pressed against his chest and legs. Sophia raised the tail of his khaki Boy Scout uniform shirt to expose his bare ass, and he heard Christine giggle.

"Now, young man," Sophia said and rested her soft woman-palm on Ben's naked ass, "you're just as much at fault as your cousin, you know." The woman cleared her throat and ran her hand over his naked bottom. Ben's prick jerked to life. With mixed feelings, Ben felt its naked length rising against naked woman flesh. Oh Gosh! He was getting hard against Aunt Sophia's naked thigh!

"Pig!" Sophia screamed and her smacked against Ben's bare ass. "Filthy little boy!" Her palm stung him again.

His prick dangled between his aunt's thighs, his balls lay in the woman's lap. From the floor, Christine's uncontrolled giggles could be heard between the smacks of the woman's hand against the boy's naked ass. Then, Sophia suddenly clamped her knees together imprisoning Ben's stiff prick between her full-fleshed thighs. The boy raised his hips and brought them down with each of his aunt's spanks, so that his dick rubbed against the soft, inner flesh of her thighs. The tip of his swollen, throbbing shaft protruded below the woman's thighs.

"Hey auntie, you got him hard," Christine piped up from the .floor. "Good for you!" Ben felt a gentle female hand cup the tip of his dick. Christine! he thought. The little bitch! But when he twisted his head up to look at her, squatting there like a monkey, her snatch wide open, he saw that both her hands were busy with her own clit Oh, Heavens! It was Sophia then!

"Can't you even control yourself when you're getting punished?" Sophia shrieked at Ben. "You pig! Why I believe you're leaking on my leg!" And she encircled his cock with one hand while spanking his bare ass with the other. Her robe had fallen open, and Ben could see her tremendous tits, naked, the nipples dark red, as she spanked his ass. Once, she let her hand slide off the burning cheeks and cup his nuts. Ben's prick was fully hard, even as his ass stung from the spanks, when he knew that all of Aunt Sophia's protestations against sex were just a sham, a cover for her unsatisfied, burning woman cunt. Sophia needed to be fucked, Ben knew, and even as she kept paddling his bare ass as if he were a little boy, he knew that he was going to be the first one to shove male gristle into her red-hot quim with its thick, black bush.

Chapter 2

Christine found Aunt Sophia's dress shop, where she had been put to work to keep her mind off "nasty filth," a bore, until a woman, about fifty years old, with a harsh, angular face, square jaw, and a slight mustache on her upper lip, came in and gave the sixteen-year-old blonde the once-over. The teenage girl, wearing, at her aunt's insistence, a dress, stockings, and high-heeled shoes to look like "a respectable sales-girl instead of a slut," recognized the hungry look in the old biddy's brittle black eyes and bent forward intent on rearranging piles of sweaters on a sales table, so that the bodice of her dress fell away from her body and the old bag got a good look at the teenager's bra-less titties.

"I'll help her, Aunt Sophia," Christine said, when she saw the tell-tale flush on the middle aged woman's cheeks, and smiled at the customer with her sweetest, girlish smile.

"I was looking for an-ah-complete outfit for my-ah-niece," the customer said with a catch to her voice, as Christine undulated towards her, thrusting her boobs against the thin material of her dress so that her nipples showed plainly.

"A complete outfit, ma'am?" Christine piped up and ran a pink tongue over her lush lips.

"Ah-yes, from the-uh-skin out, so to speak. "I-uh wonder if you could-uh-model for me, Miss?"

"Model?" Christine said and glanced over at Aunt Sophia. "Well I suppose so."

"Of course, she can and will, ma'am," Sophia said. "We have some lovely new things in lingerie."

"Yes, let's start with that," the middle-aged woman customer said. Her voice was hoarse.

"You just make your selections, ma'am, and my girl will model for you," Sophia said and pulled out a drawer from which she took several panties and laid them out on the glass counter-top.

The woman picked up three of the scantiest panties and followed Christine into the dressing room.

As soon as the customer had seated herself in a chair, her breathing heavy as if she had been exercising, Christine crossed her arms hi front, bent forward, grabbing the hem of her dress and peeled it up. The woman's breathing became more labored as the teenager's naked titties popped into view, one at a time, from underneath the rolledup dress. The teenage blonde's boobs were full and high.

"Want me to model any bras for you?" Christine asked innocently.

"No," the woman croaked. "Just the panties. Let's try these first." She held up a sheer, skimpy, triangular pair in faint powder blue.

Christine demurely turned her back on the woman and slipped her own white panties down, knowing that her naked ass was inches from the woman's face. As the blonde girl bent, lifting one leg to slip her panties off, she stuck her naked behind out at the woman customer until she felt the crack was spread wide enough for the old biddy to get a good look at her pouched pussy.

The hard-faced woman's eyes glittered as she ran her gaze over the teenage girl's creamy ass-cheeks. Her hands twitched, and the thin slash of her mouth dropped open, drooling, so that she noisily had to suck back her own saliva.

Christine turned around, now stark naked except for old-fashioned garter belt and stockings that Sophia had insisted she wear as "any decent girl would." The dim dressing room light glinted on the golden down on Christine's thighs, just above her stocking tops. The blonde girl stood slightly forward, so that her tits hung pendulously, a temptation for the raunchy woman customer.

"May I have those panties, ma'am?" Christine asked politely, a mocking smile on her moist lips, just as the woman reached for her tits. "Please, madam!" Christine said arid stepped out of the woman's reach.

"You're so beautiful!" the woman breathed. "Your breasts-"

"You want me to model the panties for you or not?" Christine said, flaunting her nakedness before the lecherous old biddy, thrusting her pelvis forward so that her pussy pouted at the customer.

"Let me put them on for you, my dear child," the woman said, "Please."

"Certainly not!" Christine acted outraged. She took the little panties from the woman and slipped them on, making sure when she raised one foot and then the other, that she showed plenty of cunt. Before the sixteen-year-old girl had a chance to get the powder blue panties up, she felt the woman's fingers sliding up into her twat.

"Oh, Jeez, how sweet!" the woman said under her harsh breath. She diddled Christine, and the teenager's cunt juice began to flow. "See how wet you are, my dear child," the woman whispered. "You want a lovely come as much as I want to give it to you."

Christine let the bag play inside of her cunt for a few seconds more, then disengaged herself from the probing fingers by stepping back.

The woman opened her mouth and stuck a thick, dark-red tongue out at Christine. She made a rapid licking motion with it and winked at the girl, who pulled the panties all the way up and struck a model's pose. "I'm good at it," the woman customer pleaded, "I can make you hear bells and see fireworks, girl."

Christine pretended not to understand. She posed prettily, swiveling about to show the biddy her ass once more. The thin material, a scant triangle, behind as in front, did nothing to conceal the teenager's pouting, plump ass-cheeks. "Do you like the fit of these?" Christine teased the woman.

"I'd make it worth your while," the woman said under her breath.

Christine cocked her head, her pretty face showed interest. The woman's eyes gleamed with lust. "Interested?"

Christine could hear Sophia come clackety-clacking toward the dressing room. "Is everything all right, ma'am?" she asked.

Christine quickly picked up her dress and covered her tits demurely, as Sophia poked her head into the cubicle.

"Oh, fine, just fine," the woman said and smiled up at Aunt Sophia. "These are really lovely, really they are. Just perfect for a young girl."

"They really are, aren't they?" Sophia said, and looked uneasily at Christine. But the teenager seemed to be a model of maidenly modesty, letting the folds of her dress cover the triangular front of her panties, showing the woman customer only a profile, her teenager's superbly modeled buttocks, setting the sheer material off to advantage.

"I'll take a dozen pairs of them, assorted colors," the customer said to Aunt Sophia. "Would you mind gift-wrapping them for me?"

"Certainly, ma'am," Sophia said. "What will you be wanting to see next? Slips? We have really a fine selection, and-"

"I'll just take the panties for now," the woman said, a trace of impatience in her voice.

"I seem to have run out of time. Could you wrap them right away? I'll come back tomorrow for the rest of the outfit"

"Of course, ma'am," Sophia said and went back into the store proper.

Christine dropped the dress and peeled off her panties. She stood before the woman, stark naked. "A car?" she whispered to the woman, "would it be worth a car to you?"

"You'll stay a whole night with me?" the woman asked.

"I'll do anything you want," Christine said.

"Oh, you lovely young thing, you," the woman whispered. "You've made an old woman very happy." She put her arms around the naked teenage girl and drew her against her dumpy body.

"A neat car?" Christine asked, her eyes large and warm.

"Anything you want, my darling girl," the woman said and cupped Christine's left tit with her hand.

Christine stuck her own hand up under the woman's dress, up the soft leg until she felt the crotch of her panties. She slid a slender, girlish finger inside of the hem and slipped it up the woman customer's cunt. It was sopping wet there. The woman kissed Christine on the mouth, her right hand hungrily stroking the blonde teenager's ass.

When the woman went down under for her cunt, Christine rolled the biddy's clit between her thumb and forefinger, and then slipped out and away from her. "We can't do anything here," the teenager said.

"Of course not," the woman croaked. "Here," she took out a card and handed it to Christine. "At my home address, tonight. I'll send a car for you at seven." She shook her legs out, held her head up high and sailed out of the dressing room.

Christine glanced at the card. It read:

Abigail Murgatroyd, Ph.D. Psychotherapy.

Christine shrugged. A cunt was a cunt. They all smelled more or less the same, no matter what name or occupation the different females professed. Quickly she dressed again and stepped out into the front of the store, where Sophia gave her a pleased smile and said that Christine had made a good start. The panties the customer had taken were the most expensive they had in the store. "Now, if you keep behaving yourself, young lady," Sophia said, "you could turn out to be quite a decent young person." The voluptuous .older woman regarded her blonde niece.

"You are an attractive girl, you know, Christine," Sophia said and quickly looked away when the teenager met her look with a knowing smirk. "Ah, what I mean is, some day there will be a young man, a decent young man, and you should save yourself for his love."

"Is that what you're doing, Auntie? Saving yourself for a special man?" Christine asked innocently.

"And why not?" Sophia countered. "What is wrong with saving oneself for the right person?"

"I thought you did not approve of any-ah-physical love," Christine said.

Sophia flushed. "There are wifely duties that a woman must perform, no matter how distasteful to her they may be," Sophia said and checked her wristwatch. She did not seem to want to continue this conversation with her niece. "Ah, I'm going out for lunch, Christine. Look after the shop, will you? And don't get yourself into any mischief."

"Yessum," Christine said and shook her head as she watched the departing figure of her aunt. Poor Aunt Sophia. She wanted to make out that she was such a prude, while all the time, under that prissy exterior, she had a yen to be fucked. Look how she held Benie's hard prick while she walloped his bare bottom. The woman was aching for prick or-? Christine smiled to herself. Maybe she wanted a gentler sort of love, a female tongue up her crack, for instance. There had been this matron back at reform school,

who had been so much like Aunt Sophia, always preaching against sex and fucking and all, until one day Christine and her friend Mercy had taken down the woman's pants and licked her cunt for her until she came so much the girls had thought she would never stop. It had been a blast. They had made the bitch beg for another pussy tonguing and made her suck the clits of the thirty girls in the cottage before letting her get off on a couple of stiff tongues again.

Christine rubbed her clit through the dregs at the thought of how well the matron had sucked it for her, rolling the pink pearl between tongue and teeth until Christine had come with such a powerful jolt, she had nearly smothered the woman between her thighs.

Christine almost wished she were back at reform school. It was not as straight as this dumb dress shop, but they were going to send her to this place for incorrigible girls, and she had heard that it was real bad there with solitary and all. Christine yawned, when a young woman came in the door. Christine looked her over, tugged down her dress and went up to her.

"May I help you, ma'am?" Christine asked.

The customer was about twenty-two or three, a pale blonde with a lovely slender body, married- because she wore rings-but looking as innocent as a twelve-year-old virgin.

"Oh, I'm just looking, thank you," the woman said and went down the aisles^ touching a dress here, a blouse there. Christine leaned against the counter and watched the slim, pale blonde nervously glance about.

"Anything in particular that I could show you?" Christine drawled.

The blonde looked at her with big, wide-open pale violet eyes. "Something in pants," the blonde woman customer said, "something not-not too loose, you understand."

"Sure, I understand," Christine said and looked the young woman customer up and down. "You're a ten, aren't you?"

The pale blonde nodded, and blushed.

Christine went over to a rack and pulled three different colors and patterns of pants out.

"How about tops? Would you like me to show you some?" the girl asked the customer.

The young woman nodded.

Christine showed her four, and the young woman selected three and followed the teenage girl into the dressing room. Christine deliberately left the curtain partly open and stationed herself where she could watch the young married woman undress.

The pale blonde pulled her dress up and off over her head, revealing modest white panties and bra. She had smooth, pale legs and nice, full boobs. When she turned to bend and pick up one of the jersey tops, her panties tightened across a lovely, highest but womanly ass. She looked so vulnerable, innocent, almost virginal. She put on a jersey top and slipped her bare legs into one of the pairs of pants. "May I check the fit?" Christine asked. "Sizes vary from manufacturer to manufacturer, you know."

"Oh, you can come in," the young woman said. "I'm decent."

The blonde teenager stepped into the dressing room and the young woman shyly avoided her appraising glance. "Oh, you mustn't wear a bra under that kind of top," Christine said with authority.

"Really?" the young woman quavered. "But I've never worn clothes just over my-ahbare skin."

"The natural look," Christine said. "Here let me help you off with this top, and we'll try it."

She pulled the young woman's top up, touching her arms and shoulders, and stepped back, holding the garment. "Just slip your bra off," the teenage girl said. The woman' hesitated. "No need to be shy, ma'am," Christine assured her. "There's nobody here but us."

The woman blushed again, but obediently unhooked her bra in back and let it drop. A pair of lovely, firm tits with pale rose nipples hung free.

"Here, let me help you with the top-" Christine began, then frowned and looked down at the woman's pants. "But no, ma'am, that breaks the lines, bunches up in the crotch-"

"What?" the woman asked confused, standing there with her naked boobs out and a pink blush on her face.

"The pants, you really shouldn't wear anything under them, if you want them to fit you best."

"Oh!" the young, married woman said. Her pale, smooth tits quivered.

"Just slip them off," Christine said, unzipped the pants, and peeled them down. When her face was even with the customer's cunt mound, Christine deliberately licked her lips.

Then she looked up into the woman's face and saw the hungry look in the pale violet eyes. "Shall we try it without the panties?" Christine asked.

"Try what?" the young woman asked hi return. Her tits quivered. She saw Christine's eyes on them and modestly covered herself with her arms.

"The pants with nothing under them," Christine said.

The pale violet eyes suddenly met Christine's. "If you think it's better," the young woman customer said and slipped her panties down her hips.

She had a pale blonde pussy, and in-the mirror, her ass shone pale and full-fleshed. The violet eyes had a wild luster in them, as the young woman exhibited her naked body to the teenage girl.

Christine reached for the young woman's tits. She cupped their resilient softness and kissed the woman on the mouth; her tongue darted between the young wife's lips, and the naked woman kissed the sixteen-year-old suntanned blonde girl back with fierce urgency. The girl fondled the pale, rosebud-tipped tits, rolling the stiffening nipples between thumb and forefinger, as the sex-starved young wife started breathing hard and pressing her belly and cunt mound against the teenage salesgirl.

Christine pulled her tongue out of the hot-tailed young wife's mouth and fastened her lips over the woman's right nipple, her tongue teasing the nub of flesh.

The young woman ground her hips against the girl's belly, and the teenager, while sucking first one tit and then the other, cupped the recently married woman's pale, plump asscheeks with both hands, drawing them apart until the rosy asshole and the rear view of her flushed and lust-swollen cunt pouch with its glistening pink slit showed in the dressing room mirror.

The randy teenage girl's long-fingered hand darted towards the exposed cunt-flesh and two fingers thrust into the warm wetness of the woman's willing slit.

"Yes! Oh yes!" the youthful matron moaned while her breath came short and hard. Her pale hands busied themselves with the bodice of the teenage girl's dress until the erect adolescent tits sprang out, naked, cream-skinned boobs with dusky pink nipples. The woman's hungry mouth sucked them, her lust fanned by the girl's ringers squishing in and out of the near-virgin cunt, so tight were its elastic walls.

"Wow!" Christine said, amazed at the woman's unbridled hands that searched under her skirt until eager fingers found her naked cunt-flesh, inflamed with lust and well lubricated with pussy-juice.

The woman had spread her legs, knees slightly bent, and rode Christine's hand as if the fingers were a man's cock.

"Doesn't your old man fuck you?" Christine asked the young woman whose ass was grinding away, the big cheeks quivering, while her cunt rotated on Christine's finger.

"Tom's away most of the time-on business," the woman said. "That's why I need, I have to-"

"I understand," Christine said and bent forward gluing her soft lips to the tender cunt.

The young woman pulled Christine's dress up, so that the blonde teenager's naked ass was exposed, the cheeks smooth and shaped like two giant hard-boiled eggs, while beneath them the cleft cunt pouch with its dark blonde bush popped out.

The blonde girl raised her mouth from the woman's cunt lips and reached for the pink hood of flesh at the top of the slit, which she squeezed until the pearly pink clit peeked out. The teenager's tongue flicked over the young wife's clit, and the pale skinned, naked young matron whinnied like a mare in heat.

Frantic for flesh, the woman reached for the girl's ass and stroked its smooth cheeks, the fingers fluttering towards the wide-spread crack, finding the asshole, fingering it vigorously.

Christine sucked the swollen clit, tonguing it, teasing it with her teeth until the young woman cried out and her cunt pulsed with a frantic come.

"My goodness! I never knew that it could be so-so-" the woman quavered.

"It's good, isn't it?" Christine said.

"Yes, oh yes!" the woman said, shuddering with breasts dancing. With two quick strokes, she stripped the slim teenager naked and drew her against herself. Tits pressed against tits, the nipples rubbing against each other. Bellies and pussies ground together. Christine skillfully fitted her clit against the young woman's and started dry-fucking her.

Moaning with pleasure, the woman sank down to the lush carpet, bucking up against the teenage girl's relentlessly rubbing clit. Christine's ass-cheeks spread wide as she dry humped the pale-skinned young matron whose own thighs opened with lust The two naked females writhed on the floor, the teenager's tight, round ass opening and closing its cheeks as she ground her clit against the woman's, feeling the soft woman meat under herself as her cunt quivered with the first spasm of a near-come. But as much as she dry-fucked the woman with urgency, feeling the tender cunt-flesh beneath her own fluttering as the woman got herself off again, Christine could not make it.

Christine stood up, bare-ass naked, her cunt lips swollen an angry red, thrusting out from her dark blonde pussy. The woman started lying on her back, her legs spread wide, her cunt slash glistening in her pale blonde bush.

"Come over here," she told the girl, and while Christine squatted so that her cunt lips, clit, and asshole were exposed and vulnerable, the young wife, turned over on her belly, her plump bottom-cheeks glistening with cunt-juice near the asshole, and stuck her tongue in between the teenager's inflamed cunt lips. Gently, but firmly, the young woman lapped the girl's drooling cunt. The woman-tongue knew exactly where the most sensitive areas were and slowly, her tongue-tip flicking at the teen-ager's clit at intervals, she brought the girl to full sexual arousal. When the woman's warm tongue rimmed her puckered asshole, Christine started to moan. The stiff tongue tip flicked up into the teenager's bum-hole, entering and withdrawing, licking at the satin-smooth intimate girl-flesh until the girl's own fingers started playing with her clit. The young woman's finely chiseled nose pressed into Christine's cunt-hole while her tongue relentlessly worked on the younger girl's bung.

This time, Christine knew that she was going to get off. Leaning forward, the blonde teenager pulled the young woman's ass-cheeks apart until the pale pink asshole lay exposed. Her naked body slithering over the woman's back, Christine licked the pale woman's cleft until her tongue found the tight bum-hole. While Christine tongue-fucked her, the woman's fingers gently found the teenager's clit, skinned back the hood and caressed it with the soft finger tips.

Christine turned the naked woman over on her back and returned to licking her asshole while the pale, young woman used her mouth on Christine's cunt. She sucked on the nub of stiff flesh near the top of the teenager's gash.

Woman and girl ate each other's meat, licking, lapping, sucking, until both were near the peak of sexual excitement. The teenager, leaning over the paler body of the woman let her nipples rub against the soft belly as she thrust her tongue hi and out of the young wife's bung.

Suddenly Christine's whole body tautened, her naked ass rose high, the cheeks wide open as she came, the woman's tongue lying way up inside of her pulsating cunt.

Chapter 3

The blonde high school girl in the short, brown, sleeveless jumper stood barefoot in the shop window, dressing dummies, rising on her tiptoes to tie a scarf over a mannequin's metallic hair. The scarf was too loose, and as the blonde, teenage girl stretched her firm and full, young body, the brown jumper rode up, revealing scant, white panties cut high, so that the base of her bottom-cheeks showed almost to the crack.

"Jeez! Will you look over there?" A boy in his late teens, wearing Boy Scout shorts, shirt and cap, shouted with excitement at his fellows and pointed to the shop window.

"Migosh! You can almost see her whole bare ass!" a young Scout piped up in a high voice.

"Boy, I'd like to shove my dick into that!" a third Scout said and sucked air in between his teeth. "Can you imagine slipping your meat into her?"

The scarf was still not right, and the young girl strained so that the muscles played under the smooth tanned skin of her beautifully shaped legs. Tiny golden hairs glinted on the swelling thighs, and the gawking Scouts could see the fine, cross grained texture of her skin, where the thighs curved up and out into womanly buttocks.

"Turn around, baby, will you, please?" the Scout who was eager to cut the girl's meat said.

The scarf finally sat on the dummy's head to the girl's satisfaction, and she stood back and regarded her handiwork with narrowed eyes, hands on sinuous hips, brown calves taut. When she stood like that, her rear towards the window, her slim back sweeping out into a deliciously curved ass, her naked legs well apart, she was the embodiment of every male adolescent's dream. Here was an athletic, sexy high school girl, her every body movement signaling her need for a stiff cock, just asking to have her legs spread and her slit reamed.

The young blonde bent forward, reaching for a handbag perched on a low shelf, and the Scouts clustering before the pane hungrily followed her every movement. Taking the purse, the blonde teenager swung around and went into a Deep knee-bend while she put the handbag besides the shoes of the manikin with the scarf. The spectators were unexpectedly treated to a view of her panty crotch, bulging with plump cunt lips, the thin, white material cutting into the slit between the swollen rolls of intimate girlflesh.

Wisps of pussy hair had escaped from the confines of the panty crotch and glinted golden above the tender inner cheeks of her ass.

The girl was either unaware of what she was showing a raunchy band of Boy Scouts or she just did not care. She kept fussing with the handbag, while the Scouts gawked at the generous display of feminity.

"Ohmygosh, my pants are splitting!" A Scout said hoarsely, as the girl finally knelt and bent forward so that the low-cut V-neck of her brown jumper fell away from her chest, and the Scouts could see her naked tits.

"Wow! Can you imagine a chick like that spreading her legs for you?" a sixteen-year old patrol leader said.

The pretty, blonde teenager's firm, pink-tipped boobs jiggled as she made some final adjustments on the window display. She shifted around so that her behind was pointed towards the boys.

"Oh baby! Couldn't we use you back at camp tonight." A young Tenderfoot said in a high-pitched voice.

The girl, kneeling, her ass towards the shop window, raised her hips, and her skirt rode up until a white triangle of panties, bulging with back-thrust cunt-pouch, pouted at the Scouts.

The Boy Scouts, their pricks stiff with longing for the thinly covered girl-meat, stared in silence.

"I bet she's just a prick teaser," the patrol leader said, his voice hoarse with lust.

"Oh, she fucks all right," a Scout with freckles across the bridge of his nose said.

"How in hell would you know, Ben?" the patrol leader scoffed at the boy who had spoken.

"I know her," Ben said. "She's my cousin Christine. I've fucked her."

The girl went into her squat again, flashing her meaty quim, the mattress of cunt-hair clearly showing through the semi transparent panties. This time, she balanced herself by thrusting one bare leg out in front.

"You fucked her?" the patrol leader said and laughed in disbelief. "Who are you trying to kid, Ben? All you've ever fucked is your fist."

The Scouts also started laughing at Ben, and the sexy teenage girl in the store window suddenly seemed to become aware of the horny bunch of Boy Scouts looking under her dress. She gave the gaping Scouts a look of contempt and clamped her knees together.

"Christine!" Ben shouted and tapped at the window, but the girl rose to her feet, and stepped back into the store, swinging her well-rounded ass. "I tell you guys, I know her!" Ben protested, as the boys hooted him down with derisive laughter.

"Sure, you know her, and you fucked her and she sucked you and I'm the President of the United States," the patrol leader said, and the boys howled with laughter.

"All right, I'll prove it to you guys," Ben said. "I'll bring her out here." He went up to the store entrance and stopped dead. There was Aunt Sophia, lecturing his cousin Christine, who was unconcernedly sitting on a chair, raising her brown jumper high up on her thighs, while she pulled a stocking on a well-shaped leg. With Sophia there, Ben could do nothing.

"What's the matter? Lost your nerve?" the patrol leader taunted Ben as he turned back from the door.

"Listen, it's true! You got to believe me!" Ben pleaded, as the walking away from the shop window, now that its main attraction for them was gone.

"You bring her to camp tonight, behind the cook tent, after lights out, and fuck her, then we'll believe you," the patrol leader said. "We'll be watching from the bushes."

"Okay, I will," Ben agreed. His prick was as hard as that of any of the Scouts who had seen Christine flaunt tits, ass, and barely covered cunt in the store window. The idea of slipping her some meat with the guys looking on excited him. "Hey! Don't you guys go and beat off thinking about her," he shouted after the Scouts. "The least I can promise you is a hand job from a real live girl."

'No, I don't want to go to any Scout campground with you," Christine told Ben three hours later. "Don't you see I've got company?"

The company with Christine in her bedroom at Aunt Sophia's was a delicious-looking fifteen year- old girl with dark reddish-brown hair, wearing a form-fitting, yellow dress with very little underneath. At least, Ben could see her boobs were hanging free, luscious jugs with large, stiff nipples showing dark through the thin, yellow cloth of the dress. Ben tried to look up under her skirt to see whether she wore panties, but the girl clamped her thighs together when she noticed his probing look.

"She can come too," Ben said, as the girl looked him up and down with an impudent smile. Ben gulped as her eyes stared right at his prick that was beginning to swell from his looking at her tits jiggling under the thin dress.

"She's Mercy," Christine said, introducing the girl to Ben. "And I'm sure she wouldn't be interested in going to any Boy Scout camp-out or whatever either."

"It's a Scout-O-Rama we're having up at the park," Ben explained. "It doesn't really get going until tomorrow morning with contests between the different troops, and demonstrations, but tonight they have storytelling around campfires and sing-along's."

"Listen, Benie," Christine said, "I saw you and your Boy Scouts when I was dressing the window over at Aunt Sophia's shop, don't think I didn't." She turned to Mercy. "Would you believe it? There they stood, gaping at me, and every one of them with his prick standing up under those silly Boy Scout shorts. Horny? I've never seen so many guys get hard from a girl."

"Umm, sounds interesting," Mercy said and ran the tip of her tongue along her up-per lip. She crossed her legs, and Ben caught a glimpse of something dark. Was it her pussy? Ben's cock tightened in his pants. Mercy was a pretty girl, and then there was something about her-her mouth. Ben thought of Mercy sucking his cock, taking the head in between her nice, soft lips and licking it with her flickering tongue. His prick crawled down his thigh until it was a powerful ridge of solid meat under his uniform shorts. Mercy's eyes were right on its outlined length.

"Why don't we go with him to that Scout thing?" Mercy asked Christine.

"You go, if you want to," Christine said. I've got to wait for Aunt Sophia." She had been glancing out of the window from time to time all along as if expecting someone. She had hardly looked at Ben all evening, and even now she seemed to take no notice of the aroused state of his prick. But not Mercy. She deliberately recrossed her legs, and this time, he clearly saw her bare snatch. The tip of Ben's throbbing prick almost peeked out from the hem of his Boy Scout shorts.

Mercy reached out and took Ben's hand and held it. Her touch made him feel warm and funny in his lower belly. "Well, I'll go with you, Ben," Mercy said. "I've always –had a weakness for campfires, toasted marshmallows and stuff." She stood next to Ben, and her hand brushed momentarily over his hard cock. Ben thought he'd shoot his load. This girl had something about her that really got him going. As she walked over towards the door ahead of him, he looked at her ass swinging beneath the thin yellow dress: nice, full, rounded cheeks, and his knees turned to jelly.

"Mercy," he whispered as soon as they were out in the hall, "Ohmygosh, Mercy." She turned around, her blue eyes wide and innocent. "What's the matter, Ben?" she asked. She came up close to him and pressed herself full-length against him, so that he could feel her tits in contact with his chest. Then she socked her belly and snatch into him. Even though it was through two layers of clothes, her quim caressing his super-stiff dong was too much for him.

"Keerist!" he breathed out and ran his hand down her back over the resilient softness of her ass. Growling like an animal in rut, Ben impatiently raised her skirt hi back and ran his hand over the naked cheeks of the girl's bottom.

The girl kissed him. on the mouth, her tongue darting against his, while he ran both his palms across her gyrating ass-globes.

"You like my ass?" Mercy whispered in Ben's ear just before she flicked her tongue into it.

"Yes! Ohmygosh, yes!" Ben croaked. "Mercy, I've got to-"

She shut him up with her mouth over his lips. "It used to drive my daddy wild," Mercy said.

"What?" Ben asked hoarsely.

"My ass," Mercy whispered and frenched his ear-hole again. Ben looked down over her shoulder at the juicy girl-cheeks. "My daddy is crazy about my ass," Mercy went on. "Do you know he gave me bare-butt spankings until I ran away from home? I mean he especially liked to make me bare it with his friends watching and all. He sort of liked to show off, make me stand there with my pants down, while he-"

"Mercy!" Ben breathed hoarsely and cupped one of the girl's ripe tits. It was firm and springy, and he felt it up, squeezing the girl-flesh, pinching the nipple gently, while Mercy ground her pussy-mound against his bursting dong. "Mercy, you've got to let me-"

"I thought you wanted me to go to that Scout thing with you?" Mercy said and broke away from Ben. She looked down at the tremendous bulge in his pants, that had leaked at its tip into a wet spot the size of a silver dollar.

Ben had forgotten completely about his promise to the troop. "Aw, heck, that can wait," he said.

Mercy reached for the steel-hard ridge of his cock and touched it with fluttering girl fingers. "Wow!" she said, "What a rod!"

Ben stumbled forwards toward her, but she ducked and eluded his embrace. Her auburn hair had fallen over one side of her face, and her blue eyes taunted him as she laughed at his condition. "You offered to take me to the Scout camp, Ben," she said, "and I want to go." She stuck her delicious, dark-red lower lip out at him in a mock pout.

"But look at this" Ben grabbed his prick. Let's take care of this first."

"It'll go down," Mercy said. She was all matter-of-fact now. "Come on, Ben, I want to see your Scouts."

Ben sighed. "Okay, Mercy," he said. He was thinking that it might even be better to take this hot-tailed little cockteaser behind the cook tent at the Scout encampment and fuck the ass off her there-with the whole troop watching from the bushes at that!

"We'll take care of that later," Mercy said and patted his bulging ridge of stiff gristle. She flicked her tongue out at him and ran down the stairs with Ben thundering after her.

"What are we doing behind this tent?" Mercy asked Ben when he had brought her to the clearing. "I thought you said there'd be campfires and storytelling?"

"Looks like we missed all that," Ben said in a low voice. "It's after lights out." The camp was quiet, except for scattered murmurs from the Scouts settling down for the night. Here and there, the remains of a campfire glowed among the tents scattered under the tall trees. A bright moon rising above the treetops lit-up the grassy patch behind the cook tent. Dark bushes surrounded this treeless area, and Ben knew that in the foliage, Scouts were breathlessly watching for his next move.

He reached for Mercy's left tit, but missed as she stepped back, pushing his cupped hand aside. "What are you trying to do, Ben?" she asked, a frown of annoyance between her arching eyebrows.

This time, Ben moved fast and grabbed a handful of tit. Mercy's palm exploded against his cheek at the same moment as a voice in the bushes exclaimed, "Wow!"

"What's going on here?" Mercy asked as there came rustling and stifled laughter from the bushes surrounding the small clearing.

"Nothing," Ben said and lunged for Mercy. He grabbed her by the hair with his right hand, unbuttoned the neck of her yellow dress, and pulled one naked tit out.

She swung her fists wildly at him, but he kept a tight grip on her hair, pulling her head back so that she could not bite him, while he mauled her large, firm knockers!, first one then the other, squeezing the springy girl-flesh, while his rod rose long and hard in his pants.

"Hey, Ben! How about letting us have a feel too?" a voice said from the bushes. Mercy struggled desperately to free herself, her bare tits quivering as she twisted and turned. She kneed Ben, driving her thigh against his hard-on, and Ben tore her dress down to her waist. He glued his mouth to one of her nipples and began to suck, feeling his knees grow weak. His grip on Mercy's hair slackened, and she tore loose from him and dashed for the bushes, right into a Boy Scout's arms.

It was the sixteen-year-old patrol leader who had dared Ben to bring a girl out here. He was stronger than Ben, and he pinioned the hard-breathing red-head's arms behind her back and held her so that the Scouts stepping out of the bushes could all see her naked tits.

"Jeepers!" a young Tenderfoot gasped, and his voice broke. The sight of a nubile girl, a pretty one at that, having her bare breasts forcefully exposed was beyond the wildest dreams of the boys clustering around her.

In the moonlight, Mercy's breasts were pale globes of female flesh, tipped with quarter sized, dark nipples. Her breath came in short gasps from her exertions, and her chest heaved, making her bare boobs rise and fall.

For a moment, the Scouts just stood there, looking. Then one of them flicked on a flashlight and played the beam over the pinioned girl's naked tits. The patrol leader held her arms far back so that her knockers stuck out like ripe melons. More flashlights came on, and Mercy's tits were brightly illuminated. Her nipples stuck out, dark pink tips on the full flesh.

"All right, you guys," the patrol leader who was holding Mercy said. "Line up for a free feel."

The boys hesitated, fascinated by the half-naked girl. Only the spots of the flashlights kept caressing her dark-nippled tits.

Finally, one Scout reached out and gingerly touched her soft but firm flesh. "Wow!" he exclaimed under his breath and ran his palm over first one then the other of Mercy's breasts.

The girl kicked out at him and her foot cracked against the fondler's left kneecap. The Scout cried out and bent to clutch his knee only to feel Mercy's shoe slam into his chest, and he toppled over onto the grass.

"Take her shoes off," the patrol leader who was still holding the girl commanded. It took two Scouts to hold each of the girl's legs while a fifth slipped her high-heeled shoes off.

The injured Scout lay on the ground, his kneecap swollen to twice its normal size. "Better get some ice for that," the patrol leader said, and a couple of boys trotted off into the cook tent.

Mercy was struggling in the patrol leader's grasp. "Let me go! Let go of me, you little bastard!" she hissed and kicked her bare heels back at the Scout's shins.

The patrol leader laughed, let go of the girl's arms, and instead clasped both of her breasts from behind. He kneaded the firm, springy flesh, pressing himself against Mercy's back, his hips rubbing against the girl's ass.

Mercy ducked, freed herself from the clutching hands, spun around, and hit the patrol leader right in the nose with her fist.

"Ohmygod! It's broken!" he cried as the girl sped away. "Catch her!" the patrol leader gasped.

"What the dickens is going on here?" a masculine voice thundered. A bright lantern threw its powerful beam into the clearing, and Mercy stopped in her tracks, barefoot, disheveled, her dress open down to her waist so that her naked tits stuck out. The speaker with the authoritative voice stepped into the clearing. He was a mature looking Scout, with masculine, hairy legs, and the shadow on his cheeks and jaw showed that he already shaved. Although only seventeen, he was senior patrol leader, and the boys of Ben's troop respected him. "You guys are making so much noise the old goats sent me to find out what's up," he said. The old goats were the Scout leaders, and some of the boys' fathers that had come along on the camp-out. Mercy noticed his eyes on her bare tits and covered them. The senior patrol leader raised his eyebrows. The girl brushed the wing of reddish-brown hair back from her face and returned his frank stare.

"We were just having some fun," the patrol leader who had held Mercy for the boys to feel up said. He was nursing his nose. On the ground, the boy with the swollen kneecap was holding a chunk of ice wrapped in a dish towel to his injury.

"It's all right," Mercy said to the senior patrol leader. "They were just trying to have some fun." She dropped her eyes and scratched at the ground with her bare toes. Then she threw the senior patrol leader a provocative look. "Only they don't seem to know how to go about it. I guess they're too young."

"Well as long as there's no harm done," the senior patrol leader said and went up to Mercy. "You're not hurt?"

Mercy shook her head so that her hair swung out about her-head. "I'd like my shoes, though," she said.

"Let's have 'em," the senior patrol leader said, and one of the Scouts handed the nigh-heeled shoes to him. Mercy slipped one shoe on, supporting herself by hold-ing on to the senior patrol leader's shoulder. When she raised her other foot to put on the shoe, she nearly lost her balance, and the senior patrol leader put his arm around her waist to steady her. When Mercy had both shoes on, the senior patrol leader still had his arm around her waist.

"Hey guys," he said, "We better move on up to the amphitheater, before some of the old goats come looking for us." he walked off, holding Mercy, who had put her own arm around his waist. Before he disappeared down the trail with her, the senior patrol leader looked back over his shoulder and winked at the boys.

"Come on," the patrol leader with the injured nose said, "let's go and get some of that ass. Old Tom will fix it for us."

Tom was the senior patrol leader's name. The excited band of Scouts took off up the trail after Tom and Mercy. Ben brushed past the boys until he took the lead. After all, he had brought the girl here, and if anybody was going to get some of her pussy, he felt that he should be first.

Ahead, he saw the glow the senior patrol leader's lantern, swinging from side to side. Then the light went off, and Ben crept stealthily ahead. When he came upon Tom and Mercy, he saw with a pang in his chest that the senior patrol leader was doing what he, Ben, had been aching to do all evening.

They were standing hi a patch of moonlight, Mercy's face turned up towards Tom, who was kissing her, long and hard. While he held her around the waist with his right hand, the senior patrol leader's left was stroking her naked tits! Tom was neither hesitantly touching the girl's bare boobs nor squeezing them as the patrol leader had done back behind the cook tent. He was massaging the girl's delicious jugs with firm, swift, circular movements that had her arching her back and rubbing her boobs against his palms, while her breath came in hard gasps.

Ben felt a painful pang of jealousy as he saw Mercy's hand with a sure move unzip the boy's fly and take out his long, stiff prick. Mercy's hand stroked the senior patrol

leader's nine niches of rock-hard gristle with experienced hands, so that Tom muttered, "Jeez!" while his cock was being handled by the girl.

Ben saw the senior patrol leader's hand slip down from the girl's naked boobs and raise the skirt of her yellow dress in front.

"He's going for her cunt!" a voice whispered behind Ben, and he saw that he was no longer standing there alone gawking at Tom feeling up the girl and getting his pecker massaged in return. The Scouts stood there, most of them rubbing their swollen dongs, aching to do what the senior patrol leader was doing.

Ben heard Mercy moan as Tom's hand started to frig her quim. "He's gonna fuck her!" an excited voice whispered next to Ben's ear, and the way Mercy kept stroking the boy's rigid cock with quick, firm jerks, it looked as if she was getting set to take it up inside her. Ben's prick throbbed painfully in his pants. At that moment he would gladly have given up ten years of his life to take Tom's place and slip his aching meat to the girl.

Ben, along with the other boys watching Tom and Mercy, tried to get a better look at the girl's cunt But although Tom's dong was clearly visible in the bright moonlight, Mercy's skirt covered her snatch. "Jeez! Look at him fingerfuck her!" a voice breathed near Ben, and Tom was doing a beautiful job of it. Mercy bent her knees and spread her bare thighs farther apart to let the senior patrol leader finger her crack. Her hips thrust eagerly up and down as she rode the Scout's stiff fingers.

Then, when Tom lost control and roughly started to force the girl towards the ground, and one of the Scouts by Ben said, "Wow! He's really gonna cut her meat," Mercy suddenly shoved the senior patrol leader back. The watching Scouts let out groans of disappointment. Tom growled and went for Mercy again, but she whispered something to him that none of the Scouts, including Ben, could hear, and he said,

"All right, if you want to," and laughed, while the girl stood on tiptoe to kiss him, her hand still fondling his erect dick.

"All right, you guys," Tom hollered, "I know you're there. Come on, we're going to have a little fun." He hugged Mercy, and she kept her hold on his prick, while they started along the trail to the amphitheater once more.

Ben and the other Scouts trotted behind them, feeling jealous of Tom, the senior patrol leader, who was getting his prick massaged by a girl's hand, while all they had were stiff peckers and the hope that maybe they were going to get a chance to rub them against some naked girl-flesh.

The amphitheater was really only a semi-circular cut in a sloping hillside, with peeled logs set into earthen terraces and a patch of bare ground at the base, where the remains of a campfire smoldered.

When Ben and the other Scouts got there, Tom was throwing logs on the red-hot embers and fanning them to a blaze with his cap. Mercy sat on one of the peeled tree trunks that served as seats around the campfire. She sat huddled forward, her face hidden by her hands, her elbows resting on her thighs.

"How many of you guys got a hard-on?" the senior patrol leader asked in a loud voice. Mercy's head perked up, and she watched the boys. Four or five raised their arms half-heartedly. "Well, okay then," Tom said, "I guess most of you aren't ready for a little fun. So why don't you all go back to your tents and forget about what I'm

showing the burly, curly-headed Scout her pussy, pushed him away and sprang to her feet on the bench.

Now, another boy dropped his pants and eagerly ran up to the girl. This one, a pale blond fellow with short-cropped hair, must have had some experience with girls before. He cupped one big cheek of Mercy's ass with his right hand, and his left went straight for her snatch. The girl bent her knees a bit and spread her legs farther apart to accommodate him. While he squeezed and pinched the full and well-rounded girlass, the pale blond Scout fingered the girl's quim. This time, the watching Scouts got a better view of the girl's snatch, as the Scout stroked the intimate groove before slipping two fingers into her.

Mercy let him feel her up until his prick stood up so stiff that it looked fit to burst, then she pushed his hands away from her body and squatted on her heels, up on the bench.

Now, more of the Scouts seemed to muster sufficient courage to expose their pricks to get a free feel. They filed past the naked, squatting girl, putting their hands on her tits, peering at her hairy twat, making a few hesitating passes at the girl-crack, and now and then slipping a boyish finger inside of her, until their peckers had risen to full hard-ons. The last one on the line filing past the girl was Tom, the senior patrol leader. He had a tremendous hard-on by the time he got to her, and, by the way in which he grabbed her by the cheeks of her ass, his fingertips digging into its crack, Mercy must have known that this mature boy would not be satisfied with a quick feel.

Tom kissed the girl again, kneading her tits, until the assembled Scouts could hear her moaning. When he stuck three fingers up inside of her, they could clearly hear the squish made by her wet cunt. Mercy groped blindly until her fingers found the senior patrol leader's cock, then she ringed it with thumb and forefinger, and gave him quick, jerky strokes that brought the organ to its greatest dimensions. Tom's prick was enormous, a veined column of angry meat.

The senior patrol leader reached around and grabbed the girl by the ass again, each of his large hands cupping one of the girl's hind-cheeks. He pulled her forward, and Mercy grabbed his shoulders for support, as the purplish-red knob of the boy's cock pressed against the elastic outer ring of her cunt-hole. As soon as the girl felt the male rod parting the wet inner lips of her quim, she tried to pull back, but the senior patrol leader forced her down, impaling her on his powerful shaft of meat. Every one of the boys watching had an enormous hard-on. This was no longer any adolescent game of touch the tittie or stink-finger. This was the real thing. The girl was being forced to take in meat. She cried out a little as she slid down the boy's gigantic shaft of stiff gristle, her moist, pink cunt ringing it like a mouth. The Scouts watched with throbbing hard-ons as the senior patrol leader unhesitatingly rammed his prick into the auburn-haired cockteaser until his pubic hair was enmeshed with hers.

Triumphantly he lifted her off the tree trunk bench, still holding her by the full, well rounded cheeks of her ass, pulling the fat globes of flesh apart so that the Scouts could see his fingers digging into the groove, the middle finger of his right hand sticking up into the girl's asshole. He slid her back and forth on his rod, which came out of her cunt glistening with her love juice, until she was lubricated enough for

"Yummy," Mercy said and stuck her bare ass out at Tom so that the cheeks parted and her hairy quim pouched out at him. While she gave the senior patrol leader a good look at her rear exposure, Mercy took the eight-inch rigid rod of the Scout who had asked for some attention into her hand, and expertly massaged it until his spunk spurted. "There, that ought to keep you down for a while," she said and watched the Scout's pecker wilt.

She went over to another one of the boys, took hold of his hard cock, pressed it against the inside of her naked thigh, and squeezed it until thick, white cum squirted out and ran down her leg. The scouts crowded around the nude girl, some pressing their erect cocks against her, rubbing against her ass-cheeks, laying their rods into the groove between them and bathing the girl's rear end with hot spunk. Mercy's hands were also busy, restlessly seeking out the firm rods of male meat, ringing them with her soft palms, and milking them with rapid, sure jerks that set semen to flowing.

Finally, her bare ass glistening from the cum that had been spilled over the tender cheeks by horny Scouts rubbing themselves against real girl-flesh, Mercy sat down on the peeled tree trunk, a stiff cock in either hand, and expertly tossed off the two boys.

As soon as she had finished with that pair, she grabbed another couple of cocks, jerked them back and forth and neatly milked the sticky cum from them.

"Hey, Mercy! Where did you learn to give hand-jobs like that?" Tom asked her. His prick hung heavy and nearly fully erect from seeing the naked girl relieving so many boys with her hands.

"Heck, I've been doing that since seventh grade to keep the guys out of my pussy," the girl said and finished off another pair. "I-" she started, but a Scout stuck the tip of his dick into Mercy's mouth and then watched round-eyed as the pretty girl tongued him, and sucked at his prick-head until he came right in her mouth. Mercy blew two more boys, expertly frenching them, so that they came quickly and completely, while a Scout rubbed his prick against her left tit until it spat white semen onto the girl's flesh.

"Hey Mercy, none of this jacking off for me," Ben said to the auburn-haired girl. "You and me are gonna fuck!"

Mercy looked at Ben's proffered prick. "You want me to get you off or don't you?" she asked and started stroking it.

"Come on Mercy, spread your legs for me," Ben said and reached for the girl's snatch.

Her hand was already milking his prick, squeezing the male gristle to make it spit.

"Listen, I wanna fuck," Ben whined. He felt a hand grabbing his shoulder.

"She doesn't wanna fuck you," the senior patrol leader said as Mercy dropped Ben's cock and grabbed the swelling meat of the older boy. She brought her lips down to it and licked its length, slowly and carefully like a little girl tonguing an ice cream cone to keep it from dripping. When Tom's tool had grown to its full nine inches, the girl stopped sucking it and knelt on the bench, her naked ass toward the senior patrol leader. She tilted her hips back and spread her thighs wide until her hairy quimpouch gaped. Then, taking Tom's shaft, she guided it in between her cunt lips, until the senior patrol leader's belly was pressing against her ass-cheeks. The boy's extended prick was lodged way up inside of her.

"Jeezus, what an ass!" Tom said and started humping the wide hipped girl. His prick slipped in and out of her fat quim, while she arched her back to spread herself as wide as possible.

Tears came to Ben's eyes as he watched the senior patrol leader again fuck the girl he had brought out here to show off before the boys. "I brought her, I should be fucking her," Ben muttered. But the boys were wrapped up in watching a girl getting fucked dog-fashion and paid him no heed.

"Harder! Harder!" Mercy cried out as the senior patrol leader slipped his glistening dong in and out of her back-thrust cunt.

Almost crying with frustration and jealousy, Ben could not watch any longer. Tucking his still-hard pecker into his pants, Ben zipped his fly, and stumbled off down the trail and back home, back to Aunt Sophia's house.

Chapter 4

"Thank you, Sophia for being so nice to me," Christine said and kissed her aunt on the cheek. The girl had come into the woman's bedroom under the pretext of wanting to talk to her. "I mean about giving me the job at the shop and all," Christine went on and hugged the woman. Sophia had been getting ready for bed and was wearing a sheer, powder-blue nightgown that set off her pale skin and dark hair to advantage.

Through the transparent material, her large, dark pussy patch was clearly visible. The teenage girl was wearing a white T-shirt that came down to the tops of her thighs, which was what she wore to bed. Sophia looked uneasy, whether because of the thick, white candle lying on the top of her dresser or because she still did not trust her teenage niece, Christine, was not sure. She put her arms around the dark haired woman's waist and pressed her slender, T-shirt-clad body against her aunt. "You're right Aunt Sophia, you know," Christine purred, "about saving oneself for the right young man, I mean." This time, the pretty blonde teenager kissed her lovely aunt right on the lips. The older woman's hands at first pushed against the girl's waist, but as the girl's lips softly caressed her own, the force of her pushing slackened. When Christine thrust the tip of her tongue into her young aunt's mouth, the woman's breathing quickened and her hands fluttered about the teenager's waist and hips.

"You're a lovely woman, Auntie," the blonde girl whispered into the woman's ear, her tongue flicking out and into her aunt's ear-hole.

"Christine, Christine, you crazy little girl," Aunt Sophia's voice was hoarse. "What are you doing?"

Christine lifted Aunt Sophia's left breast out of her nightgown and put her girlish lips over the dusky-red nipple. The woman shivered with desire. "Don't, Christine! Don't!" she whispered. But her hands went around the girl's waist and then down over her niece's hips.

"You have beautiful breasts, Auntie," Christine said, holding the woman's globular, creamy teat with both hands and sucking away at the nipple until she could feel it swelling in her mouth.

"Christine! Stop it this instant!" Sophia said, pulled up the girl's white T-shirt in the rear, and gave her niece a playful slap on her naked ass.

The girl's left hand strayed over to her aunt's right breast and cupped it, while her mouth continued to make love to the woman's left nipple. The woman slapped the girl's naked ass again, but this time, after her palm had landed, it lingered on the quivering girl-flesh, feeling its satin-soft smoothness. The woman stroked her niece's bare buttocks with both hands, pressing against the springy half-globes and finally running searching fingertips into the dusky groove between the girl's ass-cheeks. When the woman's fingertips found the girl's fleshy cunt lips, the hands stopped their searching and withdrew, hesitatingly. Both, woman and girl, knew that fingering each other's slits could lead to only one thing. The blonde teenager spread her thighs apart and arched her back so that her pretty, rounded backside stuck out, and her hairy quim-pouch became easier to reach for her aunt.

The woman's fingertips caressed the inner curves of her niece's ass-cheeks, then, as the girl gently bit her aunt's nipple, slipped down into the teenager's squishy quim. Directly, Christine began rotating her ass, so that her cunt moved against her aunt's fingers, "I don't want some nasty boy putting his filthy thing into me, Auntie," the girl whispered to the woman. "But I've got an itch, oh, my, I'm all swollen down there, I have to-to-"

"I know my dear, sweet child," Sophia breathed at her niece, while the girl rotated her naked bottom against the hand stuck in her cunt. "My, how wet you are!" Aunt Sophia said.

"Auntie, have you ever-you know-with a girl?" Christine asked the woman, her eyes round with phony innocence.

"Now, now, my child," Sophia said and started finger-fucking her niece in earnest. The woman's fingers were experienced, often-much too often-she had fingered her own burning quim to get relief. Only this was different. Here was another female, another snatch that was being reamed. The woman expertly fingered the girl's pouched cunt from behind, while her large, full tits were being sucked and caressed in return.

Christine's' right hand gently released her young aunt's left teat, and ran down the woman's body to her waist, over her belly, until it came to rest on the thick mat of mature cunt hair.

"No, don't," Sophia gasped. "We mustn't, Christine."

But she kept right on reaming out her teenage niece's back-thrust twat.

Christine moved her naked ass in wild gyrations and her fingers slid down, seeking the woman's cleft. When she found it, she was not foolish enough to go immediately for the super-sensitive clit but first to gently rub the woman's cunt lips and mound to get her whole pussy area inflamed with congested blood.

It did not take long to get the sex-starved woman hot; her moans and the sharp smell of aroused, mature cunt, told the girl that this was the time to make her move. "Have you ever had anybody lick you there?" Christine asked, while she rubbed her aunt's clit with firm, rhythmical strokes.

Sophia put up no resistance as her teenage niece backed toward the bed, bringing the mature woman with her.

The two females rolled onto the bed, fondling each other's cunt. The girl pulled up the woman's nightgown to her waist to get at her bare slit. When she had it drooling sex-juice, she scrambled around on the bed and brought her full-lipped mouth towards the woman's dark-red cunt.

Through the keyhole of his aunt's bedroom, Ben watched as his high-school-age girl cousin started to lap cunt. He had never seen two females have a go at each other, and the sight of his pretty sixteen-year-old cousin tonguing his aunt's slit further aroused his swollen prick and balls. He stroked his pecker as he looked at his girl cousin's naked ass, raised high off the bed so that her hairy, split cunt-pouch was exposed underneath her small, pink asshole. But he had seen all that before, even tasted the succulent girl-flesh. It was his young aunt's spread-open cunt that brought his male flesh to full erection.

Ben remembered Aunt Sophia, who was his mother's younger sister, as she had been nine years ago, when she had come to stay with Ben and his parents. Although he had only been six, the dark-haired, fair-skinned girl of twenty had even then given him a strange twinge hi his childish groin. He had dreamt one night of the big girl Sophia, naked from the waist down, seeing in his dream her large bare ass-cheeks. Only, in front she did not have any bush of black hair in his dream, but the hairless split V like that of the little neighbor girl he had examined a few days before.

He tried unsuccessfully for weeks to get a peek at Sophia getting undressed; then one day, he burst into her room and caught her stark naked. Her ripe boobs shocked him, but he was really stunned by the thick black bush at the base of the girl's belly. Sophia had screamed, and his mother had come rushing to take him and away chide him for entering a room without knocking first.

Five years later, when Ben had been eleven, they had gone on vacation with Aunt Sophia, who was a beauty of twenty-five at the time. Here, Ben had been able to satisfy his yen to see his young aunt bare-ass naked. The vacation place was on a farm, and there had been no plumbing. The outdoor shower stall had a hole drilled into it, whether by some resourceful farmboy who had a craving to see his sister or by a farmhand who lusted after the boss's wife, Ben did not know. All he knew, as a boy of eleven, was that there was a chance to see his young aunt stripped to the buff. He posted himself at the shower stall, being careful to hide, whenever his young aunt came out of the main house in her robe, carrying a towel. He was soon rewarded when Aunt Sophia, once inside, peeled off the robe and displayed her pale, ripe body for the eleven-year-old boy's pleasure. As she first wet, then soaped, and finally scrubbed her delicious ass-globes and teats, Ben found his pecker grow stiff, and he rubbed it with his hand, finding that this gave him pleasure. One day, while Sophia was soaping her bush, and then rubbing her hand into her crotch, Ben found that his prick had spat some sticky stuff all over his undershorts.

During the next four years, Ben often jerked himself off while thinking about Sophia all naked. As he learned more about what men and woman could do to each other to make themselves feel as good as he did when he pulled his pudding. Ben thought about sticking his rigid cock into Sophia while he tossed himself off until the spunk splashed.

Now, standing here by the keyhole of his aunt's bedroom, Ben, horny from not being able to get off at the Scout campfire fuck, suck, and feel, saw that the subject of his fist-fucking fantasies was not unattainable at all. Here was Sophia getting her pussy licked by his sixteen-year-old cousin Christine. Unfortunately, Ben could not get a real close look at his aunt's cunt, because his blonde cousin's head covered it. But

Christine's naked ass, raised up high so that and her goodies clearly showed, wasn't bad to look at either. Ben was tempted to burst in on the two females and slide his swollen prick into his cousin Christine's glistening pink cunt.

At the moment, he saw Aunt Sophia's arms reaching up and pulling the girl's naked hips down toward her face. As the boy watched, stroking his cock, his twenty-nine-year old aunt ran her tongue up into his girl-cousin's sex-slot and began to lick the cuntjuice out of the teenager's gash. Christine's ass-cheeks began to tremble as the woman sucked the girl's clit and brought her off.

Apparently, Christine had not been able to do the same for her aunt. The dark-haired woman threw her head back, her eyes closed, and her forehead furrowed as if in pain. The girl quickly got to her knees and turned completely around on the bed so that she could lie down full length against the woman's body, her clit against her aunt's. Christine mounted Sophia like a man, getting in between her spread-open thighs and starting to fuck her as if she were a man. Sophia raised her full thighs and rubbed right back.

Ben watched them going at it, girl-fucking, for a full five minutes, while he jacked off.

Then, just as he felt himself coming, he decided that there was a better way. Sophia was writhing on her bed, apparently unable to get herself off, and his cousin Christine was doing her damndest, but no matter how she humped the bare-assed woman, there was one thing that Ben could give his aunt that his girl-cousin could not: a stiff prick.

He stepped out of his uniform shorts and underpants, and wearing only his Scout shirt, walked in on his aunt and cousin.

Sophia was moaning and groaning from not being able to come, and Christine was raising and lowering her naked ass, clenching and unclenching her broad girl cheeks, to no avail. The room smelled of aroused pussy, and the sight of the two females rubbing their clits together on top of the odor, brought Ben to a new peak of sexual excitement. His prick lengthened and swelled more, and he grabbed his cousin Christine by the waist and dragged her off his suffering aunt.

"What the hell are you doing? You, son-of-a-bitch!" the girl fumed and threw herself at Ben. He lost his balance and fell to the ground, wrestling with an infuriated girl, wearing only a T-shirt that was now up somewhere around her armpits. Christine was strong. She straddled Ben, who was flat on his back, although his knees were raised, and went for his face with her fists. Her bare, wet snatch was pressed right against Ben's belly. The contact with the angry, naked girl kept Ben's prick at its stiffest as he recovered from the surprise of being attacked, and rolled over so that Christine was underneath him.

The pretty, blonde girl bit him on the shoulder, and Ben forced his knee between her naked thighs. He grabbed her by the hair and jerked her head until she opened her mouth to scream and had to unclench her teeth from his shoulder. As he wrestled her down to the floor, Ben felt his prick slide into the girl's cunt, and he rammed it in, all the way.

"Bastard!" Christine screamed, now skewered by her cousin's hard cock. As the naked girl struggled, Ben started fucking her, rolling over once more, but this time with his stiff shaft embedded in her cunt. The more she struggled, the more fun it became for Ben. Each one of her movements made his hard prick slip in and out of her twat, so that without meaning to, his cousin Christine was giving Ben the ride of his life. When the girl saw that she could not overpower her boy-cousin with sheer strength, she tried cunning: she fucked him back, moving her agile hips rhythmically and fast so that Ben found his head beginning to reel, and as soon as Christine thought her cousin had lost his vigilance, she tried to get herself unskewered from his rod. Ben grabbed her ass-cheeks and lodged his dick deep inside of her, while she pounded at his face with her fists. Ben started to fuck his cousin, harder and harder, until she stopped hitting him and began moving her hips under him. When Ben was about to shoot his spunk, Christine wrenched away and as he rolled around with her, he felt his nuts explode at the same instant that the girl's cunt convulsed and with prick-gripping spasms signaled her climax. Ben pumped what he thought must be barrels of cum

Deep inside of his girl-cousin's belly.

When he pulled out of the blonde girl and stood up, he saw Sophia lying face down on the bed, her shoulders shaking with her sobbing. Her nightgown was up above her waist and her delicious, big, white ass-cheeks lay bare for him to see.

"Aunt Sophia," Ben said, "What's the matter?"

The woman sobbed even harder. "G-g-go aw-w-w-way," she told Ben. "I'm so-so ashamed, I c-c-could die!" Her fat ass-cheeks trembled like jelly. Ben saw that her black pussy hair ran up into the crack of her ass.

Christine got to her feet, looked at the sobbing woman, pulled her own T-shirt down and went up to Aunt Sophia's head. She stroked the woman's hair and then reached for one of her big, naked breasts.

"Go away!" Sophia screamed at her. "Leave me alone, leave me alone!" and her well-shaped, bare woman's feet beat a tatoo of frustration on the bedspread. The kicking made her fat ass-cheeks quiver, and Ben's prick stirred at the sight. The idea of fucking a woman, a real, mature woman, excited Ben. He wondered if that full-fleshed delectable woman's body would feel different to his prick than the teenage girl's. He had a sudden desire to touch those woman's ass-cheeks, to run his hands over the smooth flesh and into the dark, hairy crack.

Christine looked down at the still-sobbing woman, shrugged her shoulders and headed for the door. Just before she went out of the room, she hoisted her T-shirt in the back and showed Ben her nicely rounded ass. It was small compared to the large globes of woman-flesh on the bed.

"Aunt Sophia?" Ben tried, but the woman apparently did not hear him but kept on crying. Her thighs were slightly apart from her tantrum, and Ben could see pink meat through the black tresses of his aunt's pussy. Right at that moment, Ben knew that he was going to fuck this beautiful, desirable woman. He saw his dong half-hard, and he got on the bed and lay down next to his aunt and laid his prick on her naked ass. The underside of his dick touched the cool woman-flesh, and the contact soon brought his rod erect again. Slowly, Ben started to rub his cock against his aunt's naked ass. When he saw that she made no attempt to stop him, Ben lay on top of her and reached under her for a tit. His hand found a generous boob and his prick grew harder as he cupped it.

"Benie!" Sophia cried out in alarm and turned over so that he fell off her. She looked around as if regaining consciousness and quickly pulled down her nightgown.

"Benie, I'm so humiliated," she said and started sobbing again.

"Don't be, Aunt Sophia," the boy said, "I know-how Christine is." He patted his aunt's hand.

"You couldn't help yourself, Aunt Sophia," he added and squeezed her hand. "But really it's only natural, Aunt Sophia."

"Benie," Sophia said, and he blushed as he saw her eyes on his hard prick, "You've had- ah-relations with many girls, haven't you?"

"Relations?" Ben moved his aunt's hand onto his bare thigh.

"I mean sex, Benie. I know you did it with Christine, and-oooh!" Aunt Sophia's mouth made an O, as Ben put her hand right on his stiff prick. Sophia jerked her hand away and then let it drop right back on Ben's pecker. "Thank you, Benie, for understanding," she said, leaned over and kissed him on the lips.

Ben's prick sprang to life in her hand, and she squeezed it rhythmically while she kept right on kissing him. Ben thrust his tongue into his young aunt's mouth, arid she started breathing hard. Ben reached for her tit and fondled it until she moaned. He wondered whether her cunt was already wet. My god! he thought, this is a woman, a full-grown woman, letting me feel her up, playing with my cock, and I'm going to screw her!

Aunt Sophia's nightgown was up around her thighs, and Ben ran one hand over her legs and up under it, until he could feel the tender inner cheeks of her ass. The woman slid forward until her sopping wet cunt lay against Ben's fingers. Boy! She made no bones about what she wanted! A waft of cunt odor, strong and exciting came from between her thighs. Through the tangle of coarse cunt-hair, Ben felt for his aunt's twat and slid two fingers up inside her. She jerked his prick and brought her other hand to cup his nuts, feeling his male equipment with hungry, impatient hands.

Ben finger-fucked his aunt. She leaned over and kissed him again, both of her hands now working on his prick, rubbing it, feeling it, her sensitive fingertips examining the swollen, sinuous veins, the knob, and the tip leaking clear juice in anticipation of the fucking that Ben knew would come. His tongue entwined with that of his young aunt, and Ben suddenly felt the full power of the mature woman's sexuality. This would be different from fucking a sixteen-year-old high-school girl who knew how to move her ass and cunt but had none of the powerful sexual magnetism of this woman.

"Aunt Sophia," Ben said, his voice breaking with emotion, "ever since I was six years old, I've watched you, wanted to see you naked, and I did, in the shower that summer at the farm, and Aunt Sophia, I've dreamt of doing this with you. Ohgod, Aunt Sophia, I'm crazy for you!"

Slowly, the woman leaned back, drawing Ben toward her by his prick, parting her soft, fleshy thighs until her wet, hot woman-cunt lay exposed. "Be gentle, Ben," Sophia said, "I've never- well you're the first, you know," and Ben nodded and let her slide his hard prick up inside of her, feeling the heat of her belly, feeling his balls hang against her hairy asshole.

When he was on top of her, he felt himself engulfed in her flesh, her tits under him were flattened globes of flesh, but it was Aunt Sophia's fat, round ass under him that made Ben feel the difference between this woman and the girl he had fucked earlier. She was tight, boy was his aunt tight in her snatch! And when she started to move those powerful hips, Ben started to breathe as hard as she.

Ben started sliding his prick in and out of his aunt, feeling the cushion of her ass, the limitless depth of her cunt that, however, gripped his pecker tightly and massaged its length with elastic walls. I'm fucking Aunt Sophia! he thought. My god, I'm fucking her! His strokes increased as the thought penetrated his mind that he was slipping his meat to his young aunt, making her pussy feel good, giving pleasure to that big, wonderful ass that he had seen naked in a childhood dream and later hi the shower hut at the farm. That ass was under him, bouncing him up at the end of every one of his thrusts, as the woman cried out hi her lust.

Aunt Sophia's cries of lust at first frightened Ben, but as he felt the woman rising to new heights of sexual pleasure, he became proud that he was the one feeding the fire of Ms aunt's sexual desire with his good stiff rod of male gristle. He grunted as he thrust into his aunt, watching her beautiful face, the green eyes shut, as she became lost in her bodily pleasure. My prick is going in and out of my aunt's cunt! Ben thought. Then he remembered the spanking she had given him. Now, he said to himself, you're going to pay for that! He viciously withdrew his cock from his aunt's cunt, and she opened her eyes.

"Turn over!" Ben commanded. The woman rolled over on her stomach. "Up on your knees, Aunt Sophia, and stick your bottom out."

"What are you going to do, Benie?" his aunt asked him, as she raised her magnificent bottom up.

"Legs apart, Aunt Sophia," Ben ordered. "Wider." He grabbed her large ass-cheeks and pulled them apart so that her hairy cleft showed. Her asshole winked pink through the growth of hair. Ben put the head of his cock against the pink hole and shoved. Sophia screamed in pain and rolled over on her back. "Not in there, Benie, please," she pleaded. "I'm too small for that."

"Get your ass up," Ben ordered, but this time he started to finger his aunt's asshole first. He put a little spit on his finger and started to go in and out of her tight hole, rimming it, relaxing the sphincter muscle until he thought he could try his cock again.

This time the head slid right in, and Ben slowly moved his stiff shaft, into the woman's rectal passage. "You spanked my bottom, Aunt Sophia, and I'm going to fuck yours in return," Ben said and pressed more meat into his aunt's asshole.

"At least play with my-ah-organ, Benie," his aunt begged, and put his finger on her fat twat. Ben found his aunt's clit and started diddling it, while he ass-fucked the twenty-nine-year-old woman.

He felt her fat ass-cheeks against his thighs every time he rammed his prick into her bowels. This was what he had thought of most often while he had jerked off all these years: fucking his Sophia in her beautiful, elegant ass!

His fingering of her clit brought her to renewed fever pitch and the woman started moving her big ass around and around as the boy's prick slid in and out of her butthole.

Suddenly Aunt Sophia's asshole started to contract, and she let out a loud scream as he popped off. It was too much for Ben. Here he had brought a mature woman to orgasm while he was fucking her in the ass! I'm fucking my Sophia in the ass! And with that thought, Ben spilled his load of hot, white cum way up inside of his aunt's rectum.

"Did you wash your-ah-penis, Benie?" his aunt asked him ten minutes later when he came back from the bathroom.

Ben nodded.

Sophia lay, completely naked, on the bed, her dark patch of hair starkly contrasting against the snow-white skin. "You like my-ah-bottom?" Sophia asked him.

"Ass, Aunt Sophia," Ben corrected. "I like your ass, Aunt Sophia. You've got the greatest ass in the world, Aunt Sophia. That's why I fucked you in it."

"Benie!" his aunt reproached him, "do you have to talk dirty?"

"I'm not talking dirty, Aunt Sophia, I'm telling what I did. I, a fifteen-year-old boy, fucked you, a real grown-up lady, in your rosy and tight asshole."

Sophia blushed. "It was good, Benie," her hand went for his cock. "Benie," she said, "promise me you'll tell no one, no one, about what we just did. Will you do that?"

"You mean that you don't want me to tell anybody that we fucked, Aunt Sophia?" Ben asked.

"That's right, Benie."

"Then say it, Aunt Sophia. Say what you mean."

"Please don't tell anybody that we fucked, Benie," the woman repeated and stroked the boy's prick.

"Kiss it," Ben said to her.

"What?" she looked up at him with her beautiful green eyes.

"Kiss my prick if you want to get it hard again for another go," Ben said to her.

Sophia brought her mouth down to Ben's cock and kissed it near the center of its stalk.

"The head, Aunt Sophia," Ben commanded, "kiss the head," and when she kissed it gently, he said, "not the underside of it, right where that little knot of skin is-yes!" he exclaimed as the older woman kissed the head of his prick again.

Then his Sophia took the knob of Ben's cock into her mouth and tongued it. Ben knew that she wanted more cock, and was giving him head to get it hard for him. She was not an experienced cock-sucker, Ben thought. Nothing like that little bitch Mercy or hot-pants Christine. But what she lacked in experience, she made up with enthusiasm.

Ben looked down at the twenty-nine-year-old woman blowing him, and his prick began to swell at the idea. Here was a perfectly beautiful, grown woman lying bareass naked on the bed, sucking his prick for him. Only two days ago, Ben would never have dared to imagine that he'd be lying here with Sophia on her bed, while she was using her mouth to get his prick hard enough for him to fuck her again. Sophia was really hungry for cock. She held the base of his cock-shaft and worked on the head, her cheeks sucking in with her exertions.

Sophia lay ass-up, and Ben reached over and fondled those cushions of flesh, those delicious ass-cheeks that made all the difference between fucking this woman and screwing a girl like Christine. Not that Christine hadn't been able to make him get his nuts off inside of her, but with a mature woman, a fuck was something else. Ben fingered his aunt's snatch, feeling it squishy against his fingers, and then he thought how it would feel sticking his nose up between her ass-cheeks and sniffing her hot twat, maybe even licking it for her the way Christine had been doing when he had interrupted them and won out because he had a hard cock, while poor Christine only had a mouth and a little clit.

"Want me to suck your cunt for you, Aunt Sophia?" Ben asked.

In answer, the woman spread her legs wide and knelt with her ass raised, so that Ben could slide in under her, never taking his cock out of his aunt's mouth as she blew him eagerly. Ben put his face between his aunt's thighs and sniffed Deeply. Her cunt was freshly washed, but the pungent odor of a sexually aroused woman was strong.

Aunt Sophia, I'm going to fuck you again, Ben thought, and this time I'm going to fuck that fat ass off you. He buried his nose in her hairy snatch, while her mouth did wonders with his swelling dick.

Ben sucked on his aunt's cunt-meat and tasted her. The cleft of her snatch was drooling love-juice filled Ben's mouth as he tongued her groove and then sucked on her tough, little clit. When he nibbled on her clit, the woman's belly and ass started to move in the gyrations of a fucking female, and knowing that he was about to slip meat to this woman brought Ben to a full hard-on once more.

Sophia liked having her pussy sucked though, because she kept right on working on his stiff prick while he ate her out, even reaching up and kissing her asshole. Sophia liked that because she moaned with pleasure and sucked his cock so well that Ben thought he was going to come in her mouth. He tongued her asshole, then when he felt his cum building up pressure, he pushed the woman off him, rolled her over on her back and slipped his steel-hard prick into her warm cunt.

It felt even better than the first time. Aunt Sophia's cunt gave pleasure even if Ben did not move his cock. Ben had heard older boys talking about how one girl was a better lay than another, and until now he had never understood how that could be. Maybe if a girl was especially good-looking, he had figured, she would make a better lay than a homelier one. But he had always imagined that any cunt would feel the same-like his first maybe, only warmer and wetter. But Christine had shown him that a cunt was far different and far better than a fist, and Sophia had turned out to be a most wonderful lay. When he started to rub against the walls of her .cunt-sheath, it felt so good, and Ben thought he would shoot his spunk, without having given his aunt the good cunt-reaming that she craved.

Rotating his ass, the way he had seen the senior patrol leader doing with Mercy up at the campground, Ben started fucking his aunt. This time, she folded her soft thighs around him, and he' could feel the tender, inner ass-cheeks caressing his balls, Jeez, what a woman! And it was a woman he was fucking, not a school girl. That was woman-ass there under him, grinding away, taking in his meat, while his chest pressed against the large, soft woman's tits.

Sophia moved her majestic ass slowly and rhythmically, giving her fucker the greatest pleasure he had ever felt. This woman had sucked his cock and let him fuck her in the ass, she was his exclusively. How lucky I am to have a woman, a beautiful, desirable woman-that men in .the street go hard for-as my own to fuck and suck and be fucked and sucked by in return, Ben thought, as he rode Aunt Sophia.

His prick slipped in and out of her hot, tight cunt, making his aunt moan with pleasure.

"I'm fucking you, Aunt. Sophia," Ben said. "My prick is going in and out of your cunt.

How do you like it?"

"I love it, Benie," Sophia moaned. "I love you fucking me." And she ground her magnificent ass under him so that he felt that he could not hold back any longer, and he wanted to fill this woman with his spunk. This was even better than screwing her in the ass. This woman, his aunt, was probably the best lay in the world, Ben thought, as he shoved his cock in and out of her gripping cunt.

"Give it to me! Give it to me!" his aunt urged Ben as he fucked her. "Love me! Oh, love me!" and she cried out as she started to get off, and her nails -dug into Ben's back, and her legs closed so tightly around him that he could not breathe. He kept right on giving her cock in swift, strong jabs, while she whimpered in the throes of another come, moving her naked hips under him, warm and womanish, until he could hold back no longer, and crying out, "Sophia! Sophia!" he filled his aunt's womb with spurt after spurt of hot, thick cum.

Chapter 5

Christine, wearing a low-cut, tight dress, without panties or bra underneath, pressed the buzzer under the card reading: Abigail Murgatroyd. She nervously shifted her weight from foot to foot while she waited for the answering buzzer to sound so that she could open the entrance door of the swank apartment house and go up to see the woman who only this afternoon had been so hot for her girlish body. That had been this afternoon. At seven o'clock, when Abigail Murgatroyd's chauffeur had come for Christine, she had not bothered to answer the door. Sex with the old bull-dyke had not been as appealing then as the idea of making Sophia pay for spanking her on the bare bottom like a little girl, and in front of that Benie to boot! But Christine had not been able to get Sophia off, and that jerk Benie had come bursting in and had spoiled all that.

Abigail Murgatroyd had sounded cold and distant when Christine had phoned her at nine o'clock. But she had said that it would be all right for Christine to come up. Christine was nervous, because she did not know whether Abigail Murgatroyd remembered that she had promised her a car in exchange for her ass, cunt, and tits. The pretty, blonde teenager breathed a sigh of relief as the buzzer sounded, and she went in.

The Murgatroyd woman lived on the sixth floor, and Christine took the elevator, feeling uneasy and unhappy with herself. At the age of sixteen, she already had had sex with over a hundred persons-men and woman. But with all the sex she had had, Christine felt compelled to have even more, and with new people, and although she had no trouble getting off, she had never felt completely fulfilled after a fucking or cuntsucking session.

Now, as she rang the doorbell of Abigail Murgatroyd's luxury apartment, Christine felt confident that she knew all there possibly was about pleasing another woman. She would get the old biddy to pop her ovaries a couple of times, and end up with a car to take her away from this place and Sophia who was too prissy to let herself go. She wondered how Benie had made out with Aunt Sophia. Probably had had his little ass tanned by her again. Anyway, with a car, Christine knew that she could make out. There was a whole world out there of people dying to fuck and suck or to be fucked and sucked, and a girl who was good at both could always get herself a meal and a bed to park her ass.

Abigail Murgatroyd opened the door, and gave Christine a cool, appraising look. The brittle, black eyes were hard, and the left eyebrow arched up in the angular face. The mouth curled in a sneer beneath the slight mustache. "Well, so you decided to honor me with your presence, girl?" The harsh-faced woman glanced at her large wristwatch. "About three hours late, but I guess you'll make it up to me, eh?" The woman held the door open, and Christine went inside.

The apartment was super-deluxe, with art objects, plush decor and indirect lighting. Christine glanced over at the woman's dumpy body and felt scared. Something was not altogether right here. There were two glasses on a low coffee table. Christine decided to play innocent. She looked around the lush living room with wide eyes and gave the Murgatroyd woman a winsome smile.

The biddy seemed to mellow at that and, putting a hand on the girl's upper arm, steered her over toward a wide, low couch. "What a super-neat place you've got-uh-Abigail," Christine said.

"Don't can me Abigail," the woman said, her face hard again.

"What do you want me to call you?" the girl asked and slowly licked her full upper lip.

"Mrs. Murgatroyd," the woman said.

Christine shrugged. "Okay then, Mrs. Murgatroyd," she said and sat primly on the couch.

"Well, well, well," Mrs. Murgatroyd said and put her hand on Christine's thigh.

"Oooh, Mrs. Murgatroyd," Christine cooed and kept her legs pressed together tightly.

The woman leaned over and kissed the teenage girl on the mouth. Christine struggled in her strong arms.

"Oooh, Mrs. Murgatroyd," she said, "you shouldn't. It makes me feel all tingly insidein my tummy."

The woman kissed the girl again and put a hand on her left tit. Christine made a pretense of trying to push her hand away, but then gave up and let the biddy feel her up until the woman was breathing hard. When she saw that the woman's face was flushed with lust, Christine freed herself from the stifling embrace.

"When can I have my car?" she asked and smiled sweetly.

Mrs. Murgatroyd, her eyes gleaming with desire for the girl, stiffened. "Why you little bitch!" she spat out between clenched teeth. "So you want a car do you?"

"You promised," Christine said in a little-girl manner.

"And you promised to be here shortly after seven," Mrs. Murgatroyd said. "I don't like to be kept waiting. I don't like to be disappointed."

"I'm sorry," Christine said and pouted. "I'll try and make it up to you, Mrs. Murgatroyd."

"You're damned right you will," the woman said, "if you really want that car, that is."

"Ooh, I do, Mrs. Murgatroyd, I really do," Christine said.

Mrs. Murgatroyd reached for a wall switch and flicked on a bright spotlight on the ceiling across the room from the couch. "Get over there and stand under that light," she told the girl. She herself put a light, straight-backed chair just outside of the periphery of the spotlight and sat down. Christine obediently stood in the bright light and gave Mrs. Murgatroyd an engaging smile.

"All right, let's see your cunt," the woman said.

Christine had not expected her to be this crass, and a slight frown appeared between her eyes.

"Don't you frown at me, you little bitch," the woman said. "Pull up your dress, turn your back to me, bend over, and spread your ass. And be quick about it!"

The blonde sixteen-year-old girl raised her dress, showing that she wasn't wearing any pants. Her dark-blonde bush pouted out at the woman.

Mrs. Murgatroyd snapped her fingers and made a turning motion with the index finger of her right hand. The teenage girl turned her back, showing the woman a softly rounded, pale ass above suntanned thighs. Then she bent forward. The woman studied the girl's naked bottom, noting the golden down that grew up high on her thighs, becoming slightly denser near the asshole.

"Stick it out," Mrs. Murgatroyd ordered, "way out."

The sixteen-year-old girl arched her back so that her naked ass cracked open, revealing the shadowy crevice and the cunt, pouched like a ripe and hairy fruit, split open and exposing some of the reddish meat.

"Spread your legs wide," the woman ordered the teenage girl, "and pull your cheeks apart."

Christine spread herself wide open until her inner cunt lips opened like dark-pink, fleshy petals.

The woman's brittle, black eyes glittered, and sweat beaded under the fine hairs of her mustache. She leaned forward and sniffed the girl's cunt.

"Humph, at least you're clean," she said, raised her nose a few inches and smelled the teenaged girl's ass hole. "All rinsed out, perfumed and powdered, I see," the woman said. "I bet you're not the coy little neophyte you pretend to be. Well, we'll soon see. Stay just like that," she admonished the girl who had let her ass-cheeks snap back together. "Keep showing your wares. Oh Alice!" the woman yodeled,

"come see what we have here!!

Christine, bending over, her ass-cheeks spread wide, wondered who Alice could be. She peeked back over her shoulder as a door opened and a gaunt red-headed woman with violent makeup sailed into the room.

"Ahh, Sophia-licious!" the newcomer exclaimed, her eyes on the pretty, blonde teenage girl's exposed cunt and asshole. "Nice, fresh, young meat, I see, Murgatroyd."

The red-head, whose hair stood out around her narrow, peaked face in a wild halo, took a large, round magnifying glass off a shelf and went up to the stooping, spread-open high-school girl. She leaned forward, and with the magnifying glass examined the pretty, young blonde's pouting cunt "Beautiful," she raved. "Such delicate texture, but not wet enough yet, Murgatroyd." She stuck a bony finger into the girl's open quim, reamed the delicate young flesh with it, then pulled it out and smelled it. "She's not

lubricating properly, Murgatroyd," the red-head sang out. "Think you can do anything about that?"

"You stay as you are, girl," Mrs. Murgatroyd admonished Christine, whose fingers were getting tired from holding her ass-cheeks apart for so long. The bulldyke unbuttoned the neck of the teenager's dress and pulled the two sides apart so that Christine's breasts dropped out and hung pendulously, "Lovely tits," Murgatroyd said, pursed her lips and whistled. She started rolling the sixteen-year-old girl's nipples between the fingers of both her hands.

"She's beginning to juice!" red-headed Alice shouted from Christine's backside. She again felt inside of the teenager's cunt and this time pulled out a finger that glistened with quim juice. "Here, Murgatroyd, let me relieve you," red-headed Alice said and took over from the dumpy dyke. Her bony fingers did wonders with the teenager's nipples, the quick, rolling strokes were milking the soft, swollen nubs, until Christine felt herself getting hotter by the second, despite the awkward and uncomfortable position she had been forced to assume.

"All right, baby, time for your next exercise," Alice said and raised her diaphanous robes, revealing a bright-red, dyed pussy patch, surprisingly well-shaped ivory thighs, and an almost flat belly.

"Not bad for an old crow, eh?" the red-headed woman asked Christine. "I used to be a dancer, sweetie." she pirouetted and exposed her well-defined, tight buttocks for the young girl's inspection. "See, not an ounce of surplus fat," she said. "Just enough to cover the muscle and make it soft and feminine."

"Alice, you do have a superb ass," Mrs. Murgatroyd agreed.

The red-head pulled the ivory cheeks apart, exposing a dusky-tan bum-hole. "Well here it is, sweetie," she said to the stooping girl. "That's what I want tongue-fucked." She knelt down in front of Christine, her superb ass toward the girl.

"Kneel!" Mrs. Murgatroyd commanded the teenager and slapped her across the naked butt.

Christine dropped to her knees. "You don't have to hit me," she complained. Her ass stung from the blow.

"On all fours, bitch," Mrs. Murgatroyd said to her. "You can let go of your cheeks." Alice raised her beautifully shaped rear and thrust it back until the cheeks opened wide enough to expose her asshole.

"Keep your tongue stiff, sweetie," Alice warned the teenage girl, "or mama spank."

"Start on her!" Mrs. Murgatroyd said and gave Christine another stinging slap across her bare ass to emphasize the command.

"Hey! That hurt!" the pretty, blonde teenager protested and rubbed her ass-cheeks that bore the red imprint of the woman's palm.

"That's for missing our rendezvous," Mrs. Murgatroyd said. "Now start tongue fucking."

The suntanned, blonde teenage girl knelt on all fours, her dress up above her waist, exposing her bare bottom, and stuck her rigid tongue into the red-headed woman's asshole. The high-school girl found that in order to get her tongue to penetrate the ex-dancer's bung, she had to actually press her lips against the tender, elastic ring of muscle, the sphincter that surrounded the woman's butt-hole. Only by kissing the little quivering hole was Christine able to stick her tongue a few inches into the redhead's rectum. The girl found that the exquisitely shaped woman tasted surprisingly sweet there, and the girl began thrusting her stiff tongue into the little hole with gusto.

Somewhere beneath her face, the red-head was rapidly frigging her own clit. Suddenly, Christine felt Mrs. Murgatroyd's hands on her pendulous tits, milking them with expert fingers until the teenager's cunt began oozing with sex-juice. Then, as the girl kept her stiff tongue going in and out of the ex-dancer's asshole, the bulldyke started to eat teenage pussy.

Under the bright spotlight, an attractive, blonde girl a sinuous redhead in her forties, and dumpy, hardfaced bulldyke knelt on all fours, two of them with their noses buried in another female's rear end, while the third frigged herself vigorously, her face grimacing with the intensity of her lust. In the center of the group, crouched the teenage girl, healthy, tanned, her naked ass tight, pale-cheeked, while between her thighs, her cunt-mound swelled out backwards, darker than the smooth ass-skin and furry with dark-golden hairs. This tender pouch was being expertly sucked by an experienced, middle-aged dyke, whose skilful tongue licked every nook and cranny, thoroughly sucked out every wrinkle and fold of the lust-flushed, wet, young cuntmeat.

The dancer was frigging herself with two bony, sinuous fingers, whipping the pink, pearly nub at the top of her sex-slit until it glowed red and inflamed. To complete the sensation, the sexy dancer was feeling in her vaginal area, a teenage girl's tongue stiffly moving in and out of her spread-open asshole. But with all the self-frigging and asshole tonguing, the red-head was unable to get herself off.

Furious at her failure, flushed with desire, she impatiently rose to her feet, leaving the blonde's tongue flicking in mid-air, and threw off her long and diaphanous gown.

Stark naked, the red-head flaunted her exquisite body, the tits surprisingly firm, full, and high-set.

"Murgatroyd!" the dancer shrieked, "for god-sakes get me off!"

The bulldyke stopped eating the teenager's pussy, and her chin glistening with the young blonde's love juice, puffed as she got to her feet and began to undress.

"You!" she screamed at the teenager, "get naked, quick!"

Christine hastily shed her dress and kicked off her shoes, while the dumpy, hard-faced dyke stripped down to a black corset that left her hairy crotch and large, limp boobs bare.

The dyke waddled over to the. livid dancer, and, roughly grabbing her by the cheeks of her lovely, ivory ass, thrust two fingers into the redhead's cunt, while her thumb massaged the sinuous woman's clit. "You! Girl!" she yelled at Christine, "Jam three fingers up her asshole, and be quick about it."

The teenage girl jumped at the old dyke's command, came to stand behind the writhing redhead and slid three fingers up her bung, feeling the little hole stretch and hearing the dancer's shriek of pain.

But at that moment, the red-head started to come. Her asshole contracted against

Chapter 6

"There she is! Isn't she something? What did I tell you?" the Boy Scout with a spray of freckles across, the bridge of his nose whispered to the dozen-or-so Scouts lying fiat behind a hedge with him, peeping at a beautiful dark-haired woman, elegant, and carrying her head high, clacking down the sidewalk toward them.

"Wowee! Look at them boobs bounce!" a boy burst out, and then began handling himself.

"Not so loud," another Scout said, this one with a patrol leader's insignia on his sleeve, warned.

"Hey, if she comes close enough, we'll be able to look up under her dress!" a young Tenderfoot said in a high-pitched voice. "I wonder if she wears panties?"

"She wears 'em," the boy with the freckles on his nose said. "She's a real lady. Ladies always wear pants. Only sluts don't."

"How do you know she wears pants, Benie? Huh? How would you know?"

"Because I know. I've seen 'em."

"You've seen your aunt's panties?" The Tenderfoot was aghast.

"Don't make me laugh," the patrol leader said. "Unless they were hanging out on the line."

"No, I've seen her in 'em," Ben said, "I've also seen her without 'em."

"You mean you've seen her naked, her bush and ass and everything?" the Tenderfoot asked in a high voice.

"I sure did," Ben bragged.

"You peeped at her through a keyhole then, didn't you?" the patrol leader said.

"Shh! Here she comes. Shut up you guys and take a good, long look," the boy who had handled his .prick said.

The Scouts lay stock-still watching the woman's legs. Then she was past, clacking down the pavement in her high-heeled shoes.

"Wow! Will you look at that ass? Will you look at them cheeks rub against each other?" the prick-handler said.

"It's even better bare," Ben said. "Take my word for it."

"You've never seen it bare," the patrol leader declared. "I mean your aunt sure as hell didn't just show you her bare ass, did she?"

"She sure did," Ben couldn't hold it back. "She held it up for me, and-"

"Don't tell us you fucked her hi it?" the patrol leader said.

"I did, I did. I swear it, you guys. Not only her ass, but her cunt too. I fucked her."

"Aw, come on, not again, Ben!" the Tenderfoot scoffed. "Just like you fucked that sexy blonde chick that was in that store window yesterday!"

"I fucked her too, you guys gotta believe me," Ben pleaded.

"Listen, Ben, seeing is believing," the patrol leader said. "Now Tom fucked that slut that Mercy last night. We all saw that. We saw his dick go in and out of her snatch. But you, Benie? All you did was get a feel off a her, and we all got as much."

"Listen," Ben said, "you guys wanna see me fuck my aunt?"

"Aw-come on, stop kiddin', Benie," the pecker-puller said.

"Naw, I mean it. You guys wanna see me fuck that delicious piece of pussy or don't you?"

"Okay, let's say we do, Benie," the patrol leader said. "When are you going to show us?"

"Right now," Ben said and got tip from the ground, brushing the grass stalks and dead leaves off his uniform. "I mean it, guys. You come over with me to my house right now, and I'll slip some meat to the lady."

"You're on," the pudding-puller said. "I wanna see that lady with no clothes on!"

"Hello, Aunt Sophia," Ben said as he came into the house and found his lovely young aunt busy about the kitchen. "How are you?" He still could not believe that he had fucked, butt-fucked, sucked, and been sucked off in return, by this beautiful woman. He gave her a chaste kiss on the cheek and said, "Can you come into the living room for a moment, Aunt Sophia? There's something that I want to talk to you about."

"Oh, all right, Benie," his aunt said and took off her apron. "Only I don't really have much time."

"This won't take long, Aunt Sophia," Ben said, took her by the hand, and led her to the riving room sofa. He glanced at the windows, but there was nothing to be seen. The Scouts crouching outside, just underneath the level of the sills, had strict instructions not to peep until Ben gave them the signal, which was his undershorts flung against a window pane. Shrubs fringed the frame house, and Ben knew that they were dense enough to hide the boys from people in the street as well as from the occupants of Aunt Sophia's place.

"Aunt Sophia," Ben said and put his hand out to squeeze her tit.

"Not now, Benie," the woman said. "I've got to go out"

"I've got a hard-on for you," Ben said bluntly.

"Let's fuck."

"Benie, Benie," Sophia said. "A woman needs to be put in the mood, not turned on

like some mechanical toy. You can't expect her to respond to vulgar propositions."
"But we've fucked before, Aunt Sophia. I want to fuck you again! Look!" Ben opened his fly and pulled out his half-hard prick. "I want to put this inside of you."
"Not now, Ben. Maybe later on tonight," Sophia said.
"I want to fuck you now," Ben insisted. "I want to stick my prick in between those great big bottom-cheeks of yours, Aunt Sophia."
"Don't be childish, Benie. I said not now. I've got to go and help set up the Ladies' League Charity Bazaar for tomorrow."
"You don't want to fuck with me any more then, Aunt Sophia?" Ben sulked.
She drew him towards herself and kissed him on the forehead, his face pressed into her boobs. "Of course I do, Ben, and I said, later on tonight, we can make love again." She kissed him on the forehead once more. "You are a marvelous lover, Benie," she said and got up.
Ben sat on the sofa and held back tears of frustration. There were the guys waiting to watch him slip it to Aunt Sophia, and she had to go out and help set up a Charity Bazaar! Shit!
"Goodbye, Benie," .Sophia said as she went out the front door. "Be a good boy. And keep that thing of yours for me later on tonight. Remember, it's mine, and no one else's." She blew him a kiss and was gone.
Ben stood up. Well, there was nothing else to do but go outside and face the guys. They couldn't have seen Sophia leave, as they were all hiding at the left side of the house, and the front door could not be seen from there were voices outside, high voices. Were some of the damned Tenderfeet coming in to laugh at him?
The front door burst open and two long-legged, skimpily dressed girls came bouncing in: a blonde and a pretty auburn-haired girl. "Drives like a dream, doesn't it?" the blonde said. "Hey Ben," she said to him. "Go take a look at my new car."
"Where, Christine?" he asked, and when she indicated the front of the house, Ben looked out through the window.
"But that's not a new car," Ben said.
"-and then she kept pinching my clit and I kept getting off, oh, Mercy, I tell you, it was like nothing I've ever felt before. Well it's new to me," Christine said to Ben.
"You mean she pinched it, hard?" Mercy asked her blonde girlfriend.
"She took it between her fingers and squeezed the hell out of the little thing," Christine said. "It's still all swollen and bruised. But such yummy comes. Wow!"
"We ought to try it, Christine," the auburn-haired girl said.
"That's not a bad car," Ben admitted. "How'd you get it, Christine?"
"I sucked snatch for it," the pretty blonde said.
"Come on," Ben pooh-poohed her. "Tell me, who gave that to you?"
"A dyke, a real honest-to-goodness bulldyke, Ben," Christine said.
"Let's try that clit-pinching," Mercy said.
"Okay," Christine agreed. "But go easy on mine-it's sore and tender as hell."
"How about letting Ben pinch 'em both of ours at the same time?" Mercy suggested.
"Hmm, sounds good," Christine said. "We can take turns sitting on his face."
"Hey, I don't want no dirty girl bung-holes on my face!" Ben protested.
"They're not dirty, and we'll wash 'em first, anyway," Christine said.
"I think you'll find they taste better if they're a little sweaty," Mercy said and

laughed.

"At least I like 'em that way when I give guys a rim job."

"I ain't 'licking no sweaty girl's asshole," Ben said with determination.

"But you'd lick Aunt Sophia's, wouldn't you?" Christine asked him. "Sweaty or not, you'd jump to suck her tight little hole, wouldn't you, Benie?"

"Fuck you," Ben said.

"Okay," Christine said, "fuck me." She unzipped her shorts and let them down. This time, she was wearing bikini panties, and she slipped those down her long, bare legs too.

She went over to the hall table and bent over it, sticking her nicely rounded girl-ass out at Ben. "In the ass, Ben," she said and wriggled her naked hips so that her hind-cheeks trembled.

Mercy deftly unzipped Ben's fly and took out his swelling prick. "You heard what she said," the auburn-haired girl told Ben and started frigging his prick.

She frigged good, Ben thought as his cock grew in the girl's hands.

"Wait, let me take my pants all the way off," Ben begged while the girl expertly milked his pecker with both .soft hands.

"Come on, dick me," Christine demanded from the hall table as she waggled her ass. Ben's prick jerked another half-inch in length at the sight. He stepped out of uniform shorts and undershorts.

"Hey how come you're not at that Scout-o-ree?" Mercy asked, her hands stroking Ben to a full hard-on.

"Scout-O-Rama," Ben said, "and I'd rather be doing this than tying some dumb knots." He bent down, picked up his underpants and tossed them from the hall across the living room where they thumped against a window pane and fell to the carpet.

"He's ready, Christine!" Mercy shouted triumphantly and pulled Ben by his stiff prick towards her blonde girlfriend.

"Ever fucked a chick in the ass?" Mercy asked him.

Ben nodded.

"I mean, you, know you can't just ram it up there, Benie, don't you?"

"Yeah, yeah," Ben said, "Come on, let's get started." He knew that the Scouts were watching. "Get it a little stiffer for me, will you, Mercy?" he said. Then as the girl's hand frigged him, he clutched Christine's ass-cheeks. "Put some spit on her asshole," he ordered Mercy.

The good-looking auburn-haired girl knelt down and passed her tongue up and down her blonde girlfriend's ass crevice a few times, until her saliva glistened in the butt crack.

Ben put his hard rod-head against the rim of his girl-cousin's asshole and pressed forward.

"Oww!" Christine howled. "Easy! Easy! You're so big, you'll rip me wide open!"

Ben's prick grew even bigger at feeling how tight the pretty sixteen-year-old blonde's asshole fitted around his cock.

Mercy, in a flash, stripped off her shorts and bikini briefs and slipped out of her top. Stark naked, she pressed herself against Ben's back, her cunt-mound rubbing against the boy's bare ass, and put both hands on his extended prick. Then, slowly, and ever so gently, she guided the freckle-nosed Boy Scout's erect pecker into her blonde girlfriend's elastic asshole.

As Ben sank his tool into Christine's butt-hole, he thought his nuts would pop any moment. The young girl-ass was warm, wet and best of all, tight, so that as he fucked in and out, the girl's rectum massaged his swollen rod of hard gristle.

"Frig her," Mercy whispered into Ben's ear, and flicked her warm and wet tongue into his ear-hole.

Ben's prick swelled even bigger in Christine's asshole, and the blonde girl gasped. "My god, you're so big!" while she lay bent over the hall table, her pale bottom-globes spread wide, her asshole wrapped around her boy-cousin's solid prick that slid in and out, hi and out, of the teenage charmer's bowels, "Come on, for godsakes, frig her and get her off," Mercy repeated into Ben's ear again. She took Ben's hand and guided it to the blonde's wet quim-pouch. "Rub her clit, but gently," the auburn haired teenager said and firmly cupped the boy's balls.

Ben found his cousin Christine's clit, and although she at first flinched as he touched the raw little nub, pleasure overcame pain, and as Ben rubbed the little, hard nut between thumb and forefinger, the pretty blonde moaned and ground her naked ass until Ben was about to flood her insides with sperm.

Mercy, who was squeezing the boy's nuts, sensed that he was about to spill his load, and grabbed the base of his prick and pressed hard. "Save it, Benie," she whispered in his ear, while her belly and cunt-mound rubbed against the boy's bare ass.

But the sight of his pretty, blonde cousin with her ass-cheeks spread wide, the wet, reddish-pink ring of her asshole running back and forth on his eager prick, drove Ben wild with lust. Her hairy, wet, split-open quim-pouch against his fingers, further sharpened his need to shoot spunk.

"Oh, it's so good! So good!" Christine moaned. "It's the best to be fucked in the ass! Don't stop, Benie! Don't stop!"

Ben needed no more encouragement to increase the force of his thrusts, while Mercy ringed the base of his cock-stalk, squeezing it expertly so that he was unable to pop his nuts.

From outside the house, watching the antics of the two uninhibited teenage girls with the Boy Scout, the members of Ben's troop, beat their meat openly at the sight of the hallway scene. Every one of the boys watching, imagined himself in Ben's place.

"Look at him corn-holing her, will you look at him?" the Tenderfoot said in his high voice. "He wasn't lying, was he?" the boy went on. "I mean that's that same girl we saw showing off her goodies in that store window, and Ben's dicking her, but good!"

Suddenly the pretty, blonde bending over the table to have her ass skewered, arched her back and opened her mouth in a grimace of pain or pleasure-it was hard to tell-her feet came off the ground, her legs doubling at the knees, and her naked ass bucked up and down on the table, while the boy in the Scout uniform shirt kept feeding the withdrawing meat from her extended bum-hole.

"She popped herself off," the patrol leader announced. "Now let's see what they'll do."

"That little bitch Mercy is doing something to Ben's cock," the Tenderfoot said.

"She's keeping him from shooting his load, stupid," the patrol leader explained. Then his face fell in disappointment. "Now, what the hell are they doing?" he said.

The two girls and the boy disappeared from view and the Scouts cursed Ben for a selfish bastard, for not letting them watch him giving dick to those two good-looking chicks. But their curses were uncalled for, as Ben, still with a beauty of a hard-on, and then one of the two bare-assed girls, the auburn-haired one, came into the living room-much closer to the onlookers-this time!

Mercy, patting herself with a towel between her outcurved legs, went after Ben and, holding his prick with one hand, dried it with the towel. When Christine came in and borrowed the towel to dry herself between the ass-cheeks, one of the watching Scouts said, "Looks like they washed their cunts, prick, and assholes. Wonder what they're going to do now?"

"Some real fancy sucking, I'll bet," the patrol leader said. "Watch! There they go!"

The boy, took off his shirt, and lay down stark naked on the carpet. The younger of the two girls, the one with dark-reddish-brown hair, Mercy, squatted above his head and slowly lowered her ass and cunt on his face. The boy's prick lay half-hard across his left thigh. The blonde teenage girl crouched on her knees, her upraised ass pointed towards the windows with their peeping Scouts, and gently picked up the boy's dick with her teeth. She nipped the stiffening male gristle back, so that it lay on the boy's belly, its sensitive underside exposed. The blonde ran her tongue along the lower side of the boy's prick, and it jumped more erect, glistening with the girl's saliva.

The peeping Scouts had a full view of the good-looking, blonde teenage girl's gaping cunt and asshole, and, as they stroked themselves, their spunk spattered against the wooden siding of Aunt Sophia's house. More Scout's pricks spat when Ben shoved his hand into the blonde girl's cunt-pouch and started fondling her elusive clit. He finally found it and pinched it rhythmically, while the pretty blonde girl put the swelling knob of his cock into her warm, moist mouth. Holding the straining prick with tender, caressing lips, the blonde teenager ran her tongue at the sensitive underside, about an inch from the small slit on the tip, and flicking her tongue at the sensitive underside, about an inch down from the tip, until Ben's bare hips rose and lowered, shoving the rigid cock hi and pulling out of the sucking teenager's mouth. Ben, his face smothered by Mercy's ass and cunt, smelled the full-strength vaginal aroma of a sexually aroused teenage girl, while his tongue licked in and out of the attractive auburn-haired girl's tender asshole.

Mercy was frigging her clit with firm, rapid strokes. Unlike Christine, she found that pinching the little hard noodle just plain hurt and did not give her the stimulation she needed to get herself off.

To the watching Scouts, the sight of a masturbating fifteen-year-old girl, and a good looking one at that, made their fists stroke their cocks harder and harder.

"Jeez, I want to fuck those two sluts so bad, I can taste cunt," the patrol leader said.

"How would know what cunt tastes like," a Scout peering in at the two naked girls and the boy, said and rubbed his prick rapidly with both palms.

"Why don't we just go in and fuck 'em?" the Tenderfoot asked. "That blonde, at least, has her snatch wide open and just begging for a stiff rod." He pointed at Christine's rear exposure where her pouched, hairy quim gaped, revealing the moist pink inner lining, a couple of niches below her sucked-in, rosy asshole. Her two body openings

tive spots were. The Scouts outside of the house could testify to that. When she had stroked the boy's pecker fully erect, the teenage girl, simply straddled his hips, and started sliding the stiff, male gristle in between the pink flesh petals of her cunt.

She fed herself meat slowly, lowering her naked hips until she could feel her asshole against the boy's balls. She raised herself slightly and sank down again. There were two cunts working on Ben now. His blonde cousin's was coating his nose, mouth, and chin with fresh quim-juice, while Mercy's tight, elastic cunt-sheath was massaging his erect prick.

Outside, the Scouts were about to go up to the front door, when they heard the click clack of high heeled shoes.

"It's the aunt!" the patrol leader whispered, and the boys scurried for cover.

By the time Sophia opened the gate of the low, white picket fence, the Boy Scouts were once more hiding in the shrubs, looking in through the windows, hoping that the luscious, big-assed, twenty-nine-year-old woman would strip and join in the teenagers' sex bout.

Sophia suspected nothing as she opened the front door. Then, seeing her nephew-the boy to whom she had given her cherry-sucking off her pretty, blonde niece, while that girl's friend was getting herself off on the helpless boy's prick, Sophia felt a pang of jealousy in her breast. By the time she had reached the naked, teenage trio, the woman's jealousy had turned to fury. She pulled Christine off Ben's face, grabbing the kicking teenager by her blonde hair, and then taking a handful of Mercy's auburn hair, pulled the fifteen-year-old girl off the horrified boy's cock.

"You go to your room," Sophia told Ben. "I'll deal with you later."

Holding the struggling, kicking, teenage girls by then* hair, the dark-haired woman dragged them to the phone and, taking both girls* hair into one hand, called the sheriff. "I have two juveniles here, girls," she reported, "escapees from reform school. Send someone to pick them up, please." She listened to the official voice on the other end of the line, then said, "I'll have no trouble holding them here for you," and tightened her grip on the girls' hair. She hung up. "I've a good mind to let them come and take you away just as you are," she said to the two naked teenage girls.

Chapter 7

Shortly after the bus with barred windows left town, Christine told the matron that she had to piss, and Mercy joined in that that she had to go "Number Two." The older of the two matrons said that the girls had had plenty of time to take care of these things back in town, in the jail, before boarding the bus that was to take them back to reform school. But the younger matron pleaded for them, saying that what harm could it do if they stopped at a gas station to let the girls relieve themselves, especially as they were the only two prisoners on the bus, and there was one matron apiece that could watch them and take care that they did not escape.

The older, sour matron finally agreed, and the driver pulled the county bus into a large gas station. The older matron took Christine out first, and halfway between the bus and the restrooms, the blonde teenager bolted, and made for a wooded area behind the station. Mercy, left with the younger matron, complained of cramps and threatened to relieve herself right there on the bus unless she could go to the restroom immediately. When Christine made her break, Mercy jumped off the bus and ran in the opposite direction, across the highway and into a cornfield, where the stalks were tall enough to hide her.

The matrons immediately notified the Sheriff's office, and then began to search for their prisoners. An hour later, with Sheriff's units flashing red lights and letting their sirens howl along the highway, and mounted posses scouring the countryside, the matrons admitted that it did not look as if the two teenage girls would be recaptured as speedily as they had hoped.

At the Scout-O-Rama campground, the senior patrol leader of Ben's Scout troop sat with his boys at dusk, totaling up their scores. While three of the boys started the evening campfire, the senior patrol leader lectured the boys on the importance of attending all the Scout-O-Rama events. He then read out a list of names of Scouts who had missed last night's songfest. The scheduled activity for tonight was a "Tall Tales" competition, and the senior patrol leader hoped that the boys would try and make up for last night's poor showing. "We need Ben for that," said the patrol leader who had spied on the teenagers' sex threesome the night before. "Where is Ben?" the senior patrol leader asked.

"Probably fucking his aunt," a high-voiced Tenderfoot said.

"Now that's a tall tale," the senior patrol leader said, "But let's keep it clean fellers. The judges want to hear clean, tall tales."

"Wow! Look who's here!" the Tenderfoot exclaimed and pointed towards the senior patrol leader's tent, where two dirty, disheveled girls stood watching the Scouts. "It's Mercy and the blonde!" the Tenderfoot said. "You know, Ben's cousin."

"That's Mercy all right," the senior patrol leader said, got to his feet, and went over to the girls.

The Scouts crowded behind him.

"Hey! Maybe they came to get their cunts reamed," the Tenderfoot said.

Both girls looked as if they were in need of a good bath. "Hello Tom," Mercy said and looked at the fly of the senior patrol leader's shorts.

"Listen, you girls are crazy, coming here like this." The senior patrol leader said. "You should have waited until after lights out at least."

"We aren't staying," Christine said, amused by the way the Scouts were undressing her with their eyes. "But if you guys want some real fun, come on down to my aunt's house in about an hour. You know the house where Benie is staying? Stay outside, in the backyard, until I call you."

"What are you two up to?" Tom, the senior patrol leader asked.

"Come and find out," Mercy said and ran her hand over Tom's crotch.

Sophia straddled the wash-basin and sudsed her cunt. The touch of her hand and the warm water felt good, and she caressed her thick cunt lips and pressed down on her clit. As her fingers slipped around the folds of her intimate female flesh, the good-looking, big-assed brunette started to yearn for a man. She briefly thought of the candle and the TV actor's photograph, but she knew that she needed the real thing. She wanted a prick, smooth as velvet to the touch, but hard as a rock when it slid up into her quim. After yesterday's disgraceful behavior, Sophia had punished Ben by making him stay in his room all day. She had brought him his meals, and she felt sure that after conserving his energy, the fifteen-year-old boy would be in shape to give her the fucking of her life.

The twenty-nine-year-old attractive woman dismounted the wash-basin and, holding her short nightgown up, looked over her shoulder at the reflection of her large, white ass in the mirror. She would let the boy feel up her cheeks until his prick stood up.

Then, she would let him rub her breasts and finger her cunt until he couldn't control himself any longer. Only then, when his prick was hard and swollen with blood, would she let him put it into her twat. She would make him fuck her again and again, until his prick couldn't get stiff any longer. Her hand pressed against her cunt-mound with desire. She needed cock-now!

Barefoot, her full, pale legs flashing below the transparent nightgown, the voluptuous woman, her ass hot for a man, opened the door of her bedroom and started down the hall toward her fifteen-year-old nephew's room. She was halfway there, when a board creaked behind her, and she swung around and saw her niece Christine standing there, looking at her with a mocking smile.

"Hi, Aunt Sophia," the teenager said. "Where are you going in such a hurry?"

"You?" Sophia gasped. "You're supposed to be back in reform school."

"But we're not," a voice said from behind, and Sophia looked back at Christine's friend Mercy. The auburn-haired girl had an unsheathed Boy Scout knife in her hand. "Now you just get that nice, big ass of yours downstairs," she said.

"I'll call Benie," Sophia said. "Benie!" she shouted.

"You got him locked in there, Auntie," Christine said. "We tried his door."

"Yeah, Christine and I were going to blow him in turn, take all the starch out of him," Mercy said. "What did you do, keep him locked up so he'd be good and horny for you?"

"I'll take the key to Benie's room," Christine said and held out her hand.

Mercy brandished the hunting knife. "Let's go or I'll start cutting," she threatened.

Sophia handed the key to Ben's room to his sixteen-year-old cousin.

"Downstairs," Mercy said threateningly arid put the point of her knife against Aunt Sophia's back. They marched her into the living room.

Once in there, Christine and Mercy burst out laughing. "Oh, Auntie!" Christine said, "you didn't really think we'd hurt you, did you?"

Mercy tossed the knife behind the couch.

Sophia looked puzzled. "You mean you're not angry at me for having turned you over to the Sheriff?" she asked.

"No, not at all, on the contrary, Auntie," Christine said and hugged the delicious, full bodied woman.

"How did you girls keep from going back to reform school?" Sophia asked.

"That's a long story, Auntie," Christine said and kissed her aunt on the lips. She rubbed her tits against her aunt's and found the woman was kissing her back. Christine felt her aunt's big, beautiful tits. She fondled the nipples and fingered them gently until they swelled.

Mercy put her hand between the two embracing females, raised Aunt Sophia's short nightdress and felt her cunt. As the woman, started breathing hard, Mercy gave her two fingers up the wet snatch, while Christine pulled her aunt's nightgown up over her head so that the twenty-nine-year-old woman stood stark naked before the two teenage girls.

Mercy kept working her fingers in the woman's cunt, and Christine caressed her aunt's ripe boobs, until they gently got her down on the carpet. While Christine pushed her aunt's legs up towards her chest, Mercy put her soft, pink lips to the woman's randy cunt and started to suck. Her mouth worked up and down along the woman's slit, licking the clit and reaming the cunt-hole, making passes at Aunt Sophia's exposed bung from time to time, until the voluptuous, dark-haired, naked woman started to rotate her wide hips and moan for relief. Mercy fed her a stiff tongue, while her supple fingers frigged the woman's clit. Sophia moaned with pleasure.

Christine went to the kitchen, unlatched the back door, threw it open, and ran back into the living room. She held Aunt Sophia's wrists over her head and ran her mouth over her full tits. Mercy grasped the twenty-nine-year-old woman's ankles and pushed them up so that her dark-haired crotch was spread wide.

The beautiful, dark-haired, twenty-nine-year-old woman lay on her back, her legs up, so that between her fat, white buttocks, her lust-swollen cunt gaped.

Mercy used her lips and tongue again on the woman's open, pink-petaled snatch. Aunt Sophia's white belly heaved as she waited for the telltale flutterings of a big orgasm. She closed her eyes to let it come and did not see the Boy Scouts trooping in, gaping with wonder and lust at a mature woman's fully displayed sexual equipment. The sixteen-year-old patrol leader was the first to drop his pants. He gave his half hard prick a few strokes and knelt between Aunt Sophia's upraised thighs. Then he lifted his prick and laid it into the groove of her gaping cunt. Aunt Sophia's eyes opened.

She knew that this was no longer the tongue of a teenage girl that touched her sensitive private flesh. She struggled against Mercy's and Christine's restraining arms, and the desperate movements of her big ass let the patrol leader's cock slip into her. At that moment, as she felt hard, male flesh sliding up her quim, Sophia heard muffled grunts and, turning her head back, saw her fifteen-year-old nephew Ben, gagged and trussed being carried into the living room. In spite of the boyish prick starting its strokes in her tight cunt, the woman noticed that her nephew had been expertly tied up. His wrists had been fastened to his ankles, and a baseball bat was thrust behind his knees so that he was helpless. A Scout neckerchief gagged him. A big boy, the senior patrol leader, and another older Scout carried Ben down by his aunt's bared, spread ass, so that he could watch her getting fucked.

Tears of anger and frustration filled Ben's eyes as he saw the patrol leader raise his narrow, boyish ass and bring it down between his aunt's spread thighs. A pang of jealousy shot from his groin to his chest, as he realized that he no longer was the only male to have tasted Aunt Sophia's delicious cunt. The patrol leader was grunting with pleasure as he threw long, slow fuck strokes up the beautiful woman's hot, wet cunt. But he had no control, no endurance. His small hips bobbed up and down, faster and faster as the full, mature, woman-hips brought him nearer and nearer to shooting spunk.

"Poor Benie," Christine said and undid his pants. "You didn't think you could keep Auntie as your own private stuff forever, did you?" The pretty, blonde girl pulled the fifteenyear- old boy's pants down low enough so that she could get her hand on his prick.

"Poor Benie," the sixteen-year-old girl repeated and with three firm strokes of her soft hand made her cousin's prick get hard. "Doesn't it excite you to see Auntie getting fucked?" Christine teased her cousin and stroked him to a full hard-on.

Ben, groaning through his neckerchief gag, found that with Christine's hand stroking his cock, he was getting aroused by the sight of a boy slipping meat to a twenty-nine year- old woman. The patrol leader was fucking like crazy now, while Sophia struggled against the two Scouts who had relieved Christine and Mercy of the task of holding her arms and legs.

The boy between Aunt Sophia's legs pushed his ass way down, so that Ben knew his prick slid far up inside of his aunt's quim, and then fucked rapidly, like a dog. Suddenly, he raised his head. "Aaaah!" he yelled, "Aargh!" and his ass-cheeks clenched.

"He's filling her full of spunk, Benie," Christine said and started nibbling with her lips at the tip of Ben's prick. Ben found that the touch of his pretty girl cousin's warm, wet mouth on his cock, coupled with the sight of his young aunt getting fucked by a boy in a Scout shirt, made him want to get his nuts off. Christine, feeling his need through his swelling prick, started to stroke him off with her mouth. She gave him an expert blowjob, soft mouth, gentle lips, and a constant tongue massage. By the time the Tenderfoot mounted Aunt Sophia, first feeling up her ass and tits to get himself hard, Ben let his nuts pop into his cousin Christine's eager mouth. The blonde swallowed his cum and pulled her mouth off his cock, sucking the last drops of spunk from the tip before letting it pop out of her lips. The teenage girl smiled at her cousin.

"That was quite a load, Benie," she said and patted his balls. A thin siring of spunk hung suspended from her glistening lower lip to the tip of Ben's prick.

"My turn," Mercy said, and took Ben's softening tool into both her hands, and started caressing the male sex flesh. The girl's touch coupled with Sophia lying stark naked on the carpet, spread wide by four Boy Scouts while a Tenderfoot tried to find the right angle of the luscious woman's cunt sheath so he could stick his prick in for his first piece of ass, excited 'Ben.

"Aarrrgh!" Sophia cried out as the Tenderfoot shoved in manfully but not up her hole. Christine went over to the fumbling boy, stooped quickly, bending her knees, and taking hold of the boy's stiff cock, guided it into the woman's cunt-sheath. "Noooo!"

Sophia wailed as the boy fucked her like a jack-hammer. He was out before he even got a chance to feel the inside of the ripe woman's cunt canal.

"Shit!" the Tenderfoot cursed and tried to get back in.

"Easy does it," Christine said and taking up his stiff prick, gave it a few flicks to get it harder and shoved it back up into Aunt Sophia. "Don't fuck so fast," the pretty blonde teenager said to the Boy Scout who was tasting his first piece of pussy. The Tenderfoot started fucking like a rutting dog again, and Christine reached down and held his hips and showed him how to go in and out slowly. "Let her feel you," she advised the boy. "You bang away fast and shoot your load, and she won't even know you've been inside of her."

Mercy had hand-stroked Ben's cock to semi-hardness, and now she started licking it like a little girl licks a rapidly melting ice cream cone. Here and there, Mercy tongued the boy's prick, jerking it now and then to get it harder.

The Tenderfoot was getting the hang of it and savored the feeling of his cock embedded in warm, moist female flesh.

"Mygosh! He's only a child!" Aunt Sophia, screamed and struggled against her captors.

The Boy Scouts kept her right on her back, legs up and over her boobs, arms straight out at either side of her.

"He's fifteen," Tom, the senior patrol leader said. "Same age as Ben, and we know you've been fucking for him."

Christine, squatting down, watched as the Tender-foot's small ass clenched and unclenched as he fucked. He suddenly let out a high-pitched shout, and the pretty, blonde girl reached in between his straining legs and cupped his balls as he came. She felt the boy's nuts up until he lay still, and the teenage girl knew he had stopped spurting cum into her aunt.

Mercy had gotten Ben hard and was giving him a first-class blow-job. The auburn haired girl ate cock, sucking and licking to coax the sperm out of the trussed-up boy's dong. Ben was beginning to sweat as his heart pounded in the throes of intense sexual arousal again. While the good-looking girl worked with lips and tongue on his prick, Ben saw another Scout slipping his meat into his gasping aunt.

"How's your fuck hole, ma'am?" one of the Scouts holding Aunt Sophia's legs asked her. "Oughta be getting warmed up pretty good with all that cock you're getting. Bet you've never had so much meat so fast, eh?"

Her new fucker was a pimple-faced boy who growled as he slipped his long, angry red prick into Aunt Sophia's spunk-filled cunt-hole. He knew how to fuck though, and he rotated his bare ass while he jammed his prick in and pulled it back out of the beautiful woman's gash.

Ben came painfully into Mercy's caressing mouth. The girl sucked every last drop out of him, making his orgasm last and last as her sucking brought on more and more spasms. "No more, no more! Mercy, please!" Ben yelled, his lean belly heaving with a final spurt of cum. His gag had slipped down from his mouth.

Sophia was beginning to moan and breathe hard as the pimple-faced boy gave her long, lingering fuck strokes that went Deep inside of her belly.

"Yes!" she said, "yes!" as the Boy Scout made her feel that she was getting her cunts heath reamed out for the first time that evening.

Christine relieved Mercy with Ben and started fingering his cock. "Hey, Mercy," the blonde girl said, "come and help me get him naked. We're going to have to suck his asshole and nipples in a while to make him get it up again."

Mercy leaned behind the couch and retrieved the Scout knife that she had used to threaten Aunt Sophia. With the help of the knife, the two girls stripped the fifteen-year old boy naked, without disturbing the ropes that trussed him in a helpless and completely vulnerable position. They stood him on his knees, his face against the carpet, and then reaching from behind, Christine found his dick and started milking it with practiced hands. "He's got about two, three full loads left," Mercy said, expertly feeling the boy's balls. "Then it'll take some doing to get him to spunk."

"Leave me alone! Stop it! Stop it!" Ben shouted as Christine's experienced fingers brought some stiffness to his hanging meat.

"Gag him, will you Mercy?" Christine said. Her hands made slapping sounds as she stroked the boy's prick. The auburn-haired girl untied the Scout neckerchief from around Ben's neck and retied it tightly, the cloth cutting into Ben's mouth. He could only grunt as his pretty girl cousin milked his prick down as if it were a cow's udder. Mercy stood and watched with fascination as the boy's organ swelled under his girl cousin's expert caresses. Ben stared with impotent fury as the pimple-faced boy got Sophia hotter and hotter. He felt ashamed that he could not help his aunt and that his genitals were being handled by the two sluttish girls as if they were just so much male meat to be made stiff and milked of all gism. The tight ring of Christine's index finger and thumb moved slowly down his stiffening prick. The blonde girl's left index and middle fingers felt the tip of the organ with their soft pads. "He's starting to lubricate again," Christine said in a professional manner. "Come on, Benie, give me a nice mouthful of your hot spunk, will you?" She pulled her cousin's half-hard dick out between his buttocks in back and, lifting the balls off it, ran her lips along the underside of the organ.

With short, quavering shouts of ecstasy, Sophia came as the pimple-faced Boy Scout expertly kept fucking her. The Scouts, watching the beautiful, mature woman getting fucked, gaped with awe as her ripe body trembled in the throes of female orgasm. "She's a hot one," Tom, the senior patrol leader said. "Keep on fucking her, she'll get off again."

But the pimple-faced Scout feeling the sexual heat of the climaxing woman's cunt, could no longer restrain himself. With a hoarse cry of pleasure, he pumped his sperm into her belly. He was still shooting the sticky, white stuff, when Tom pulled him off the woman, and giving his own nine-inch cock a few flicks to get it as stiff as possible, the senior patrol leader mounted Ben's aunt. "I'll have her coming again," the senior patrol leader boasted, and his muscular ass tightened as he slipped his meat into the woman.

The pimple faced Scout, thick, white semen leaking from his still-hard prick, cursed Tom.

"Here, let me help you," Mercy said, knelt down, and drank in his drippling cum. The pimple-faced Scout grabbed the auburn-haired girl's head, shoved his prick in her mouth and finished himself off. Without batting an eye, Mercy swallowed his sperm as it erupted into her mouth.

Christine had kissed Ben's prick into a nice hard-on. Now, she was getting down to some real fancy cocksucking. Holding the boy's sex organ by its rigid base, the blonde teenage girl used every trick she had learned to make him shoot off into her caressing mouth. The teenager made love to the boy's prick with her lips and tongue and the soft, inner pads of her cheeks. She gently bathed the swollen organ with her spit, keeping it moist and warm, while she searched out its most sensitive spots to apply tongue and lip pressure. But whatever caresses her tender teenage lips bestowed on Ben's pecker, her whole mouth kept up an uninterrupted stroking, a rhythmic milking that she knew would eventually make him get off.

The senior patrol leader fucked Sophia with all the knowledge of his seventeen years, and he seemed to have plenty. He brought her to her second climax with half a dozen or so powerful fuck strokes. The woman whinnied like a mare as she popped her twat.

"Let me go! Let me go!" she breathed at the boys holding her.

"Let go of her!" the senior patrol leader ordered without breaking his rhythm. As soon as the boys released her, Aunt Sophia's soft thighs and calves embraced the boy servicing her, and her big, fat ass started to move. "Jeez! How sweet it is! Oh, how sweet!" Tom sang out as the woman's arms went around his waist and her boobs rubbed against his lower chest. Ben could smell the odor coming from Aunt-Sophia's sexually aroused cunt as she was being screwed. As he watched her taking on the big senior patrol leader, his nuts triggered for the third time, and Christine got a throatful of hot sperm. She smiled in satisfaction at her success, and used her tongue and lips to draw sperm from the boy until the last drop of the orgasm had been drained from his cock. "Phew!" Christine exclaimed, her lips glistening with spunk, a trickle of the sticky, white stuff hanging from her chin. "It's getting tougher, Mercy."

"I've never sucked a cock yet that didn't spit," Mercy bragged. She handled Ben's nuts and semi-soft prick. "Come on, Benie, let mama have some of your nice, delicious love stuff." She fondled him, and he started to get hard in spite of himself.

With great skill, Tom brought Sophia to the brink again. The woman moaned as she felt the male meat rubbing against her cunt sheath. He drew his long prick almost completely out of the woman before slamming it home into her again. She came with a loud outcry and dug her nails into Tom's shoulders. Her big ass thrashed about, and it became too much for even Tom. Shouting, "Take it! Take it, you horny bitch!" the senior patrol leader shot spurt after spurt of spunk into Aunt Sophia's cunt.

Benie, kneeling with his thighs apart, his face pressed into the carpet, struggled as Mercy rubbed his hardening prick between both palms, quickly and firmly, until it stood up. When she began caressing his organ with her mouth again, Ben's muffled groans of protest only increased the vigor with which she stroked him with mouth and hands.

Sophia was being ass-fucked by a Scout who had long lusted after that tight, little hole. She had simply brought her legs up again and the boy began to corn-hole her. Aunt Sophia's hands kept the boy from plunging in too rapidly. Once he was in her asshole though, she fucked him as she had fucked Tom, rolling her hips and giving him the ride of his life.

The patrol leader, who had been the first to fuck Aunt Sophia, approached Christine, his cock hard as a rock again. "Come on, baby, let's fuck," he said to her, swaggering a bit. He still could see the blonde teenager as she had teased the Scouts in the window of Aunt Sophia's shop in his mind, and now this same girl had just finished blowing her fifteen-year-old cousin, and he wanted to fuck her.

Christine shrugged and slipped off her shorts. She let the boy pull up her top so that he could get at her breasts, and while the patrol leader felt her tits to get himself aroused to peak hardness, Christine fondled his prick. When he was ready, the blonde let herself down on the carpet, spread her legs, knees up, and let the boy enter her.

She fucked him skillfully, returning thrust for thrust.

"Mmmm! Mmmmm!" Ben protested as Mercy sucked his cock with vigor. She had pulled it back underneath his buttocks and caressed it like a ripe fruit with tongue and lips. Although swollen to full hardness, Mercy knew that she would have to work a bit harder to make the boy get off again.

Sophia felt hot spunk explode up inside of her rectum as the butt-fucker got himself off. As soon as he pulled out, a new boy took his place between Aunt Sophia's thighs and slipped his erect prick into her. He was not prepared for the fierce heat with which the mature woman demanded sexual satisfaction. The boy, a Second-Class Scout, had thought that it would be like fucking his fist, only wetter and warmer. But this was a live woman under him, not a cunt without a body or brain, and she wanted him to give her pleasure. The Scout fucked away bravely, while the woman's cunt devoured his piercing prick.

The patrol leader shot cum into Christine's cunt, grunted and pulled out of her. Christine paid him no further heed. "How's it going, Mercy?" the blonde, asked her girlfriend who was blowing the trussed-up, naked boy.

"Almost," Mercy said and worked on Ben with her hands. She milked him, and then took the knob of his dick into her mouth. She knew just the right amount of pressure to give, and the boy popped off. His watery spunk spurted into Mercy's mouth. Christine immediately started on him again. She licked her fifteen-year-old boy cousin's asshole, and then kissed and sucked his nipples. Finally, she took the boy's balls into her mouth and gently rinsed them in her saliva. When she touched his prick with her tongue, it slowly began to swell. As the blonde high-school girl gently began to work on the boy's prick with her skilled tongue and lips, the naked, trussed-up male began to cry.

The Scout fucking Sophia came, pulled out, and another boy took his place. This one managed to bring her off before he had thrust into her more than three times. But he kept on fucking her, aroused by her orgasm.

Ben, his mouth gagged, his arms and legs tied with expert Scout knots, sobbed as Christine gently brought him to full sexual arousal again. The blonde looked with pride at the boy's long prick. She knelt behind her naked, fifteen-year-old cousin, who was trussed ass-up, forehead on the floor, and pulled the webbed Scout belts from the uniform shorts that she and Mercy had cut from his body. From her position, Christine could see Ben's asshole and below that his healthy, firm balls. Milking the boy's prick with her left hand, the lovely sixteen-year-old girl doubled the web belt and very softly hit the boy's balls with it. She kept up the gentle blows.

Sophia never knew that it could feel so good to constantly have a stiff prick rubbing away inside of her cunt. The boys, lined up to get a piece of ass off her provided her with fresh cock that could keep her near the peak of sexual arousal and bring her off every few minutes. The boys' faces and bodies blurred and became just one to her, one male with a hard dick, who fed it to her tirelessly. As she gasped in the throes of another climax, Sophia was certain that heaven had to be like this. It was the best feeling that a woman could ever experience, and she wished that it would never have to end.

As a new boy slipped his hard prick into the beautiful woman's wide-spread gash, her young nephew writhed with the first spasm of yet another orgasm. To bring it on, his teenage cousin Christine had stuck her finger up his ass and expertly massaged his prostate until that, and her other hand firmly milking his prick, brought on a dry, nut popping come. Immediately, Mercy relieved her girlfriend, and putting Ben's soft dick completely into her mouth, nurtured it back to a semi-hard-on again. Sophia had been fucked by every Scout of Ben's troop. And now, Tom, the senior patrol leader, had two Scouts take her to the bathroom to rinse out her cunt that was brimming with sperm. When the naked woman came back, led by two Scouts, Tom's wicked hard-on greeted her. The senior patrol leader lay down flat on his back and had Sophia mount his erect cock. Then, as the Scouts watched, the mature woman started fucking the boy.

Ben watched his aunt sliding herself up and down on the Scout's thick shaft as the cramps of yet another orgasm gripped his nuts and asshole. He saw his young aunt throw her head back and ride a hard prick as if it were a bucking bronc. Then, as she shrieked out her pleasure at yet another orgasm, Ben saw the room beginning to spin. It spun faster and faster, and then stopped, upside down, and then everything went black as the boy fainted.

Chapter 8

When Christine spotted the black-and-white patrol car, it was already too late. The deputy sheriff must have been keeping pace with her as she walked toward town for at least several minutes-long enough to get a confirmation of her description, and the fact that she was wanted for two successful escapes from custody. Christine walked a little faster, and the black-and-white also speeded up. Damn! Why did she have to give in to her body? Why couldn't she control her animal appetites?

The pretty, blonde, sixteen-year-old girl had left Aunt Sophia's house to get herself a man-a real man, not some silly and horny Scout. She was on her way to the seedy side of town, where she was sure she could find a guy with enough balls to give her what she needed. And now, this damned sheriff! Christine glanced over her shoulder and saw him: mirror-lensed sunglasses, broad-brimmed hat, everything she hated. She ducked in between a frame house and a tall, unkept hedge and started to run. Her short skirt let her really move her bare legs in long, running leaps. That she wasn't wearing any panties, in anticipation of the tough, muscular guy she had hoped to meet in a bar in the tenderloin district, didn't bother her now. She would shake this dumb deputy, shake the whole damned stupid town with its wooden-sided frame houses, neat, white picket fences, and Scout-O-Rama in the park on the outskirts.

The blonde teenage girl ran across an empty lot and towards a field of tall-stalked corn. Out of the corner of her eye, she saw the blur of tan before she even heard the heavy thumping of the deputy's running feet. He was shouting at her, ordering her to stop. Christine ran, even though she felt the sudden pain of a stitch in her side. She was across the lot, leaped a low hedge and crossed a grassy patch of an abandoned shack, when the beefy deputy grabbed her and brought her down, rolling over and over, her short skirt high. His face was red with exertion, his sandy hair disheveled as he hugged the lithe teenager and took the handcuffs from his belt. Christine unzipped his fly and took out his cock. It was uncircumcised, and the girl skinned back the foreskin, jerked the male meat a couple of times so that it sprang up stiff and fat in her fist, and slipped it into her cunt.

The deputy tried to get loose, to pull himself out of her snatch, but at the same time, he went for her wrists, so that he could get the cuffs on her. By the time he got both of her arms behind her, Christine was using her hips so expertly that at the same moment that he clicked the handcuffs on her, the deputy swore and a great rush of hot spunk came inside of the teenaged girl's belly.

"You horny little bitch," he said and tucked his pecker back inside of his pants, so that he could march her back to his black-and-white like a proper sheriff. A thick wad of spunk slid down the inside of the girl's leg as the deputy guided her to his patrol car. When he brought her to the sidewalk, people had gathered around his car, and they looked curiously at the deputy sheriff leading a pretty, blonde, teenage girl to his car, her arms handcuffed behind her, and thick, white spunk running down the inside of her left leg and down into her shoe. When the deputy looked down at his pants, he saw with embarrassment that there were pecker tracks on his fly.

He drove the patrol car away with a squeal of tires and put on his red light and siren. "Now what did you have to go and do that for?" he asked his girl prisoner.

"I wanted you. You turned me on," Christine said. "Didn't you enjoy it at all?"

"You're a hot-tailed little piece all right," the deputy said. "And if I wasn't on duty, I'd play that game with you all day and night."

"You're the best hunk of man-meat I've ever had," Christine said and kissed the red necked deputy on the cheek. "Do me again, will you please?"

"You're nutty," the deputy said and glanced sideways at the pretty teenage girl who was his prisoner. "What in hell did you go and run away from reform school for?"

"My daddy put me there, said I was incorrigible," Christine told the deputy. "Only he was lying. It was because I wouldn't let him fuck me any more that he did that."

The young deputy sheriff shook his head. "And your momma? Didn't she try and help you?"

"My momma's dead," Christine said. "I've got a stepmother, and she didn't try and help me at all. She'd laugh and watch my daddy fuck me. She'd even hold me, if I wasn't of a mind to."

"You poor kind," the deputy said and patted the teenage girl's bare thigh.

"Wanna fuck me again?" Christine asked him, a teasing smile on her glistening lips.

"Look, I gotta take you in," the deputy said. "You understand that, don't you? I mean I'm on duty and all, and-"

"Sure, I understand," Christine said and slid down low in the front seat of the police car so that her skirt rode up and the hair between her thighs showed.

"Pull your skirt down, will you please?" the deputy asked her.

"Why? Does it get you hot?" Christine looked and saw the telltale bulge in the young deputy's pants. "Listen you," she said. "I could marry you, and then the court would turn me over to you, put me in your custody or whatever, and we could fuck each other all the time."

"Now you cut that kind of talk out, youngster," the deputy, who was no more than four years older than his girl prisoner, said.

"I've never fucked anybody as good as you," Christine said and kissed the deputy on the neck. "You could drive off to the side road," she said, "and fuck me one more time before they send me back to reform school. You don't even have to take the cuffs off.

Just take out your cock and slip it to me."

"You want to marry me just to get out of going back to reform school," the deputy sheriff said. "For no other reason."

"Wanna bet?" Christine asked, and leaned down and gently bit the bulge in the deputy's pants, "Hey! I can't go into the station with a great big hard-on and bring in a young female prisoner that ain't wearing no pants," the deputy said. "They'd think I took your undies off and played stinkfinger on the way down there with you." Cutting the wheel sharply to the right, the deputy drove the patrol car onto a dirt road and up into the woods.

He unzipped his fly and his prick sprang out, big and hard and uncircumcised. Christine, her arms handcuffed behind her back, leaned forward and used her teeth to skin back his foreskin. She gently coated the knob of his cock with saliva. "Wanna put it inside of me?" she asked, her eyes wide and innocent "More than anything else in the world," the deputy said and reached for the teenage girl's cunt.

"You'll marry me?" Christine asked, and kept her thighs pressed tightly together. The deputy's prick stood thick and long, the foreskin revealing the moist, reddish knob. "Let me put it inside, please," the man pleaded.

"Promise you'll marry me?" Christine asked again.

"Okay," the deputy blurted you. "I'll marry you. I'll marry you, just let me-let me-"

"Sure," Christine said and spread her legs wide and put her feet up on the car seat. The deputy's hand went for her snatch, came out wet, and he took out the keys for the cuffs. Christine turned her back to him to let him unlock the cuffs. "Listen, you won't be sorry," she said. "You marry me and I'll blow you every morning before you go to work. I'll blow you when you come home, and the rest of the time, I'll spread my legs for you, like this." The pretty sixteen-year-old girl spread herself wide.

The man unbuttoned her blouse, took out a tit and bit it gently, while Christine guided his stiff prick into her teenage cunt. While he started to fuck her, Christine took her index finger, slipped it up his ass, and felt for his prostate. When she had located it, she dug her nail into the gland through his rectum, and triggered his spunk.

The young man shouted in surprise and joy as he emptied himself into the young teenager. He kept shooting spurts of spunk into her for two minutes, while her nail pressed his prostate. "Gawd, you're the greatest," he said to the girl. "I've never, never-"

"You're getting hard again," Christine said, "I can feel it." She moved her bare ass on the plastic seat in the front of the black-and-white patrol car.

"It's gonna be all right, baby. Everything's gonna be all right," the deputy said as he started to fuck the pretty, blonde girl again.

Mercy watched the men coming out of the hotel: old men, young men, middle-aged men, and then there was the help. She ignored the latter completely. The others were salesmen, retired men, nondescript men, and idle men. None of them would do. They didn't have enough money. In brief shorts and a halter top that left her midriff bare, the fifteen-year-old girl slowly paraded her stuff. Chest out to make her titties stand up and out, and swinging her hips to call attention to her best feature, a gorgeous, beautifully rounded ass, Mercy strutted.

Men looked at her, some winked, others made remarks. Mercy ignored them, and turned away. From time to time she yawned. She watched the men getting into then: cars. Here were four that had a brand-new sedan. But four men just wouldn't do. If some eligible guy didn't come along soon, the damn sheriff's guys would probably spot her, pick her up and send her back to reform school, the same way they had treated Christine. Mercy figured maybe she'd better try her luck with truck drivers, although they sure as shooting didn't have the kind of money that she was after. She started down the street, away from the hotel, when she spotted him. He was about fifty-five, silver hair, distinguished-looking, and his clothes were expensive. Mercy knew about men's clothes and how to spot winners and avoid losers. This guy was definitely one of the winners of the world. He had the bellman drive his car up for him, tipped with a couple of bills, and was about to get into the new, sporty, luxury car, when Mercy caught his eye. He seemed to lose his cool self-possession when he took in the scantily dressed teenage girl, but recovered quickly and slid into his car.

The engine purred to life, and he was about to pull away from the curb, when Mercy sauntered over and casually asked him if he was going out of town.

"As a matter of fact, I am," he said. "But why are you asking me?"

"Because I need a ride out of this town, mister," Mercy said. "Want some company?"

"How old are you?" the man asked skeptically.

"Old enough," Mercy said, and walked around the front of the car, opened the door and slipped in beside the man. He cleared his throat as she sat up close to him, and glanced down at her bare leg. "You like my legs?" Mercy asked him and stretched them out stiff.

The man drove off. He drove down the highway, letting Mercy chatter about how she was looking for a guy with money to get away from the boring town, and how when she found a guy like that, there wasn't anything she wouldn't do for him.

"Anything?" The guy asked.

"Anything," Mercy assured him. "Why? What have you got in mind?"

The guy cleared his throat. "Ever posed for any photos?"

"You mean nude?" Mercy asked back. "Well, yes, now that you mention it."

"Yeah," Mercy said and licked her lower lip. "I did that for a while. Beaver shots and all."

The guy grew red. "Any–uh–films?" he asked her.

"Yeah, I had a bit part in some fuck film," Mercy said. "Why, are you a movie producer, mister?"

"Ah, well, not, not exactly," the old guy said. "But I am what you call a very keen amateur photographer and cinematographer. An-ah-serious devotee of the film arts."

"Sounds real neat," Mercy said. "Is that your line of work? Because I'm thinking of taking up acting and stuff."

"Uh, that's great, heh, heh, I mean, I'm in business, but I'm thinking of devoting more and more of my time to photo and movie work. And sooner or later-who knows?-I may need a sexy little actress like you."

"Listen, mister, I can show you how good I am in front of a camera," Mercy said.

"Good, good," the man said. "I can give you an audition right now. Just say the word."

"You mean right here? On the road?" Mercy asked, "No, of course not. But I've got a place-uh- about half an hour from here. Want to come and try your luck?"

"I'm game," Mercy said.

Half an hour later, the car pulled up before a large, secluded estate house. "Wow," Mercy said. "Is that yours?"

The guy nodded. "It's one of the places I own," he said.

Mercy knew she had hit the jackpot. "You mean you've got more places like this?" she asked him.

"Not like this, but I've got-oh, about six or seven-in a couple of cities, and then in Europe." The man led her to the front door.

"You got a wife?" Mercy asked bluntly.

The guy shook his head. "Never got around to that," he said.

He took Mercy upstairs, letting the fifteen-year-old girl lead the way, and she knew he was getting a good eyeful of her girlish ass. On the second floor, the guy had acomplete, professional photographer's studio. He flicked on a couple of floodlights.

"Now, if you will," he said.

Mercy hooked her thumbs into the waistband of her shorts, popped the snaps, and pulled them down. She turned her back on the guy, giving him a good eyeful of naked ass, while his camera whirred and clicked, whirred and clicked, as he took pictures of her. He used strobes as he photographed the half-nude teenager, who spread her buttocks apart for him, and even knelt down to give him a full rear view of her split beaver, bunghole, and ass.

"Listen, you got the job," the guy said to Mercy as he loaded his motion picture camera.

"What job?" Mercy asked.

"I need a full-time model," the guy said. "I take an awful lot of pictures here-only for my own amusement," he said.

"What do you do with them? The pictures?" Mercy asked innocently.

The man grew red and stammered something about art and the beauty of the female form. But Mercy would not let him off that easily. She wanted to see some of the films he had taken, and the guy finally could not resist her begging. He pressed a button so that a screen came down from the ceiling, and pulling up two chairs, he set up a projector, loaded it, and after switching off the lights, started screening.

His films were of girls. It was always the same treatment. A girl, a waitress in one film for instance, would appear, smile, and start to strip. When she had her snatch bare, she would spread it and show pink, moist flesh. Then there were the ass shots, and finally the girl would masturbate herself to a twitching climax.

As the guy watched, he seemed to get more and more excited. He licked his lips,

Chapter 9

Ben watched Sophia putting away the groceries. She was wearing a thin, silky, brown dress that showed off her ass to full advantage. Under the chocolate brown material, the big globes of ass-flesh trembled, contracted as she reached up high into a cupboard, and rubbed against each other when she walked. The rich color complemented her fair skin, dark hair, and green eyes. Unaware that her fifteen year- old nephew was watching her body as it moved, the attractive woman leaned over to pick up a brown paper bag, and Ben could see down the front of her dress, her full and juicy-looking boobs. As he looked at this woman, who was his aunt, his mother's young sister, the boy still could not believe that not only had he fucked this self-possessed woman, but he had seen her bare-assed naked, taking on a whole troop of horny Boy Scouts. She had spread her full thighs for them, revealed her black-haired beaver and the split, ripe, fruit-like cunt.

Sophia kicked off her shoes and stepped on a stool to put away a can of coffee. As she rose oil her tiptoes, Ben watched her skirt ride up above her knees while the muscles in her calves tightened and accentuated the sexiness of her woman's legs. When next, the twenty-nine-year-old woman, who was his aunt, bent, her ass held out towards him, Ben's pecker had grown stiff with longing. He wanted to screw this lovely, grown-up woman. A week ago, if he had seen a beautiful woman like Sophia and gotten hard from looking at her body, Ben would have only one source of relief: jerking off. He would have run into the bathroom and, while thinking about the woman naked and how it would feel to fuck her, he would have rubbed his stiff prick until the spunk came. Now, Ben knew that he did not have to toss himself off to get rid of his hard-on. He could stick it into the beautiful, mature woman, into

the globes of flesh against his naked hips and thighs. The woman stuck her ass up higher so that she could get more prick in with every thrust.

"Harder, harder," the woman pleaded with the boy. "I'm nearly there, Benie. Come on! Split me open! That's it! Give it to me. Give it to me-Arrgh!" His aunt moaned and bucked her ass as she got off.

Without missing a stroke, Ben kept on fucking her. She was better, if anything, since her gang-banging by the Boy Scout troop. Having lam naked while boys fucked her one after another, then-companions looking on, had removed all inhibitions from the ripe woman. She wanted-she demanded-sexual gratification from her fucker. Ben, for his part, had learned to control his spunk. He could hold back and give a cunt the reaming it deserved. He could give a woman pleasure and make her lose her senses as she came, crying out in her lust, her cunt-flesh twitching with the spasms of the female orgasm.

After getting herself off, Sophia turned over on her back and grabbed Ben's still hard prick and put it back inside herself again. The twenty-nine-year-old woman was now lying on her back, her knees drawn up, her dress bunched up above her waist, while between her naked thighs, her fifteen-year-old nephew was rendering her stud service. Sophia raised her naked legs up as she ground her hips and slowly drew the hot sperm from her nephew's balls.

Ben gave a hoarse cry and let go. He felt his spunk erupt and flood his aunt's inner belly. With the image of her lying there, naked from the waist down, bared just for him to gain access to her secret flesh, her juicy cunt, Ben emptied his nuts complete-ly into his aunt's cunt hole.

"You're the best," Ben told his aunt a few minutes later, while he dried his prick on a dish towel. "I mean there couldn't be any other woman or girl better than you, Aunt Sophia."

His aunt was wiping between her legs with another kitchen towel, and Ben watched her thick growth of cunt-hair, black and coarse, against the "white linen.

"Benie," she said, "you were my first lover. And nothing can ever change that. You're a wonderful boy, and I'll spread for you anytime, but Benie, I'm going to have to try some men. I've never fucked a grown-up man, do you know that, Benie? Now don't you look so downcast, Benie. You're only fifteen, and a boy. A very mature boy and a wonderful sex partner. But Benie, in the long run, it might be better if you tried fucking some girls your own age."

"I did, Aunt Sophia-Christine and Mercy-but let me tell you, you're the best, Aunt Sophia. When I fuck you, I never want it to stop."

"I'm flattered, Benie," Sophia said and tugged her chocolate brown skirt down over her naked ass and belly. "But your parents are coming back tonight, and you're go-ing home with them. You may want to visit me once or twice a month, and maybe we'll have a good fuck once in a while." She stroked his hair. "But Benie, I don't want you to be jealous. I can't be exclusively yours. It's high time, I tried it with a man."

Three days later, Sophia was sorry that she had ever said those things to her young nephew Ben. Since he had left, she hadn't as much as seen a boy's, let alone a man's, cock. And she was aching to have somebody fuck her. She sat on the sofa in her living room and fingered her clit. She had frigged herself to orgasm at least a dozen times since her nephew had gone back home. It was no good, she thought, as she put her bare feet up on the couch, spread her thighs, and used her finger on her clit. She rubbed the little nub while she thought of men's cocks, all big, all swollen with hard-ons, all belonging to men just dying to get them into her hot, twitchy twat.

It was no good-she needed more than her finger now, she needed more than the candle that lay forgotten upstairs in her dresser drawer, a poor substitute for the real thing. A few times, she had tried to pick up a man, but the ones she had seen had done nothing for her. Almost crying in frustration, she pulled her dress back down and thought about a hot tub-bath, when the front doorbell rang.

Standing on the front stoop was a young man in the greenish-khaki uniform of the Boy Scouts. He wore long pants and had a green tie instead of the neckerchief the boys all wore. "Hello, ma'am," he said haltingly. "I'm Bob Shepherd, Ben's Scoutmaster. May I come in?"

Sophia hoped that he couldn't smell her finger. She wore a green dress to match her eyes, and it set off her fair skin and dark hair to advantage as as had the chocolate brown one. She was barefoot, and that made her feel vulnerable, and she rubbed one bare foot with the toes of the other.

"May I?" the young man repeated. "Or if you prefer, we could, of course, talk right here-"

"Of course, come in, come in," Sophia said. Looking down at the young Scoutmaster's crotch, she opened the door wide to him. He seemed to have a nice fat and long cock from what she could tell by the bulge running down the inside of his left thigh. His ass was small and muscular, Sophia noted, as he went across the room. "What can I do for you Mr.-ah-Sheppers?"

"Shepherd," the youthful Scoutmaster corrected her. "This is sort of awkward for me, ma'am," he said. "You see there've been complaints-some of the parents of the boys in our troop."

"Complaints?" Sophia repeated. She tucked her legs up on the sofa, knowing that she was showing a lot of bare thigh, and that her legs were good. "What kind of complaints, Mr. Shepherd?"

The young man sighed. "Well for one, there are reports that a couple of girls, one of them your niece, I believe, tried to be forward with our boys. Now, we try and discourage any sort of unclean thoughts among the boys. In that way, we hope to eliminate-ah-self-abuse."

"Self-what?" Sophia asked, although she knew very well that the young man was talking about the boys jerking off.

"Ah, masturbation," the Scoutmaster said.

"What have a bunch of little boys pulling their puds have to do with me?" Sophia asked.

The young man blushed at her language. "To be frank ma'am, there were some of the boys who told their parents that you let them-ah-take certain liberties with your ah-person."

"You mean that I let them feel me up?" Sophia asked.

"I believe that was what they were referring to. I cannot believe that you would have allowed it to go any further."

"You know, you're not bad-looking," Sophia said. "Not bad-looking at all.

"Ma'am?" the Scoutmaster stammered.

Sophia got up from her sofa and walked over toward the Scoutmaster. She moved her body sensuously, seeing his eyes on her bra-less tits. When she got right up to him, she squatted down, keeping her bare knees together, but knowing that the hem of her dress fell away from her ass and thighs, and that the man, if he cared to look, would see that she wasn't wearing any underwear. She took up his limp hand in her own and put it palm out on her right breast.

"Ma'am," the Scoutmaster said and had trouble swallowing. "Ma'am, you're the most beautiful woman that I've ever seen."

Sophia put the Scoutmaster's hand inside of her dress and let him feel bare tit. She watched with pleasure as his pants began to tent. In another five minutes, she'd have this succulent young man fucking her. Reaching out, the woman unzipped the young Scoutmaster's fly and took out his swelling prick. It was a nice big one, and Sophia kissed it and started to mouth it, while the Scoutmaster began to breathe hard and, although feeling her tit, said*, "Ma'am, please."

"Come on," Sophia said to him, "let's clean your plumbing out."

"Ma'am, I respect you," the Scoutmaster said.

"Don't tell me you're a virgin?" Sophia asked him and then bent back to sucking his stiff prick.

"No ma'am," the Scoutmaster said. "But you're the mother of one of my boys-"

"Aunt," she said. "I'm not Benie's mother, only his aunt."

"Oh, that's better then," the Scoutmaster said and looked down at the beautiful woman who was licking and sucking his cock.

"Come on down on the floor with me," Sophia said and pulled the young Scoutmaster out of his chair by his hands and on top of her lush body.

She let him lie against her until she felt his pecker twitching, then she extricated herself, rolled the young man over on his back, undid his belt, and pulled off his trousers and underpants. He had a luscious pair of big balls under his thick prick. Sophia knelt and mouthed it again. When she could taste his first juice in her mouth, she shifted around until her knees were one at either side of his head, so that the youthful Scoutmaster could see and smell her cunt. She pulled up her dress, high, before taking his stiff prick into both hands again and sucking it with a vengeance.

"Oh, god that's good!" the young man cried out, and found that the woman was lowering her body, her hairy, strong-smelling snatch for him to eat. The Scoutmaster had eaten cunt before, but none as delicious as Aunt Sophia's. This woman's box was something special. Of course it wasn't the gash alone, it was the idea of seeing this lovely woman's cunt bare and lubricating, ready for prick. The Scoutmaster ran his tongue along the groove of Aunt Sophia's cunt, and she started to move her nice, full hips with passion.

Eating a man, Sophia found, was different from eating a boy. The man smelled stronger, a pungent scent came to her nostrils from the young man's balls. Then there were the hairy legs and ass and the beard stubble that prickled her cunt as the young man sucked her sex box.

Even as she blew him, bringing his dick to the full stiffness necessary for good fucking, Sophia knew that this would be a superb fuck. She could hardly restrain herself. She wanted to take the young man's prick inside of herself, let it love her and rub her until it erupted. In wonder, Sophia looked at the big balls-those were man's balls-and suddenly Sophia learned that she was dealing with a man this time, not an inexperienced boy.

The Scoutmaster reached up and pulled the woman's big buttocks apart. Then, pressing his face into the intimate flesh of her crotch, he started to drink in great mouthfuls of her cunt liquids. When he was ready to fuck, he upended the woman, keeping her dress high, laid her on her back, and knelt between her legs. He felt her breasts up until she began to moan, then slowly but relentlessly he entered her. His prick slid in between the pink, fleshy petals of her cunt lips, and up her snatch. Sophia humped.

She wanted cock, and this was it! She moved her powerful ass, and the Scoutmaster knew that he was getting fucked. He knew that this was a woman whose ass he was cutting. Slowly, he fucked her with all the expertise he could muster from having screwed about two dozen girls and women. He was going to make her pop her ovaries off, and more than once!

The woman embraced him, bit his ear, called him "lover" and drove him wild with her lust. She fucked as if she hadn't had cock for years! But he knew that a good-looking woman such as this must have had plenty of pricks shoved up her.

Sophia opened herself up, shamelessly, she spread herself wide to let this young man taste the full fire and .sweetness of her womanhood. Her twat, her belly, her asshole, the entire groin, pelvis, and crotch were swollen with lust, as she took on a man for the first time in her life. Sophia enjoyed the feel of his body on hers, the strength of his prick as it stretched the elastic lining of her cunt-sheath, as it made her feel so completely a woman. She moved her big ass, giving the man fucking her as much pleasure as she could, and getting all she could out of this-the best piece of man's tail, any woman could ever dream of having. Crying out her delight, Sophia got off, feeling her pelvis pop with the spasms and flashes of a good, full come.

This was different from the many small comes she had gotten when the Boy Scouts had gang-fucked her, it was different from the nice orgasms that she had experienced with Benie. This was Deeper, fuller, more lasting. She howled her lust out as the Scoutmaster caught her fever and let his prick spurt cum. As Sophia clutched him with her magnificent legs, her ankles crossed in the small of the young man's back, and she received the love spunk of a man only seven years younger than she was.

"All of it, lover," she urged, humping while the Scoutmaster kept pumping his cum into her.

As she stretched languorously after the best fuck she had ever had, Sophia knew that this young man was going to service her often and fully.

Briefly, she wondered if Benie had found a girl to give him what he needed yet.

Chapter 10

Ben watched his prick grow bigger under the warm spray of the shower. When it was semi-hard, he started to beat it. All the time that he was stroking himself off, he thought of girls, older girls, and women, like Sophia. He thought of Sophia putting out for Shepherd, his Scoutmaster, and became jealous. The Scoutmaster had a terrific collection of fuck magazines and books. They showed men and women doing it in all sorts of positions, and he probably was teaching Sophia some of these kinky things. Ben wanted to fuck, he didn't want to have to beat off like this.

He felt ashamed and disgusted with himself. Just a few days ago, he had all the ass that he could handle: Sophia of course, and then there had been Christine and Mercy. But now, he had only his fist to give him relief. Sophia was into men. He'd seen her downtown a couple of times with some real old guys, guys with grey hair and all-that was when she wasn't running around with that horny Scoutmaster. Ben wished that Christine had stayed in-town, over at Aunt Sophia's. The blonde had been a good piece of tail-not as good as Sophia maybe-but she had always been good for a quick fuck to take the edge off his rut. Then there had been Mercy, who had a lovely little ass that wouldn't stop. Well they were both back in reform school now.

Christine had been picked up a couple of days ago, and he'd heard only yesterday how Mercy had been found about a hundred miles away, on the highway, standing by an expensive car with a guy behind the wheel who was dead-heart attack, they said. Mercy had been taken in by the state police, and it was just a matter of minutes until it became known that she was wanted for escaping from reform school.

Ben let the warm water caress his dick, closed his eyes and thought of a girl, a lovely girl, a few years older than he was. The kind of girl who never gave him a tumble. He thought of such a girl, naked and spreading her legs for him, and his hands started to stroke faster and faster, when-

"Benie! Benie!" It was his mother.

Damn! He couldn't even get himself off in the darned shower any more.

"Benie, I need you to go over to the market for me, hurry up," his mother said through the door.

The store! There was nothing more boring than the damned store. And soon it would be back to school and the same stupid routine. Ben finished showering and dried himself. He would run away, first chance he had. Go somewhere where he could get ass whenever he needed it. He put on his underwear and went to his room to dress.

Twenty minutes or so later, over at the supermarket, Ben was buying a pound of hamburger, when somebody behind him said, "I wish I knew how to make good stew."

Ben turned and saw this girl: long, dark hair, nicely fitting jeans, boobs that would make good handfuls. She must have been talking to somebody, a husband or boy-friend or another girl. She was about twenty-two or so, Ben figured, nice ass, nice legs from what he could tell through the jeans.

"I do so hate eating hamburger every day, don't you?" the girl said.

Ben looked around, and there was nobody there at the meat counter but he and the girl.

"I don't like hamburger much either," he said, "but my mom-" he shrugged.

The girl gave him a warm smile. "I know how it is," she said.

"Listen," Ben said, "I've got this recipe for stew, from the Scouts, and it's real good, if you'd like, I could-"

"Sure," the girl said, opened her purse and took out a small pad and a pencil. "Would you mind?"

Ben wrote the Scout recipe for stew down for her. When he gave the pencil and pad back to her, his fingers touched hers and she gave him another encouraging smile.

"Well, thank you," she said and wheeled her carriage away.

At the checkout stand, he bumped into the girl once more. Again, she smiled, and Ben asked casually, "I could cook that stew for you, you know. That is if you want me to."

"I'd love that," the girl said.

Ben followed her outside and found that she had a neat sports car. She drove a few blocks to a nice apartment house, and they went upstairs.

Ben prepared the stew, put it on the fire, and found the girl in the living room.

"By the way," the girl said, "my name's Penny."

Ben introduced himself. "That stew'll take another couple of hours," he said. "I guess I better go now."

"You don't have to," the girl said.

"Then I won't," Ben said. "What would you like to do?"

The girl looked him up and down. "I don't know. Any suggestions?"

"Well, depends on what you like," Ben said. "You like to fuck?"

"Yeah," the girl said, "but I'm really into multiple orgasms, and I find that most guys can't do me enough to give me more than three."

"What guys have you been doing it with?" Ben asked.

"Oh, just guys and a couple of profs over at State College. I'm a senior there."

"I can get you off six, seven times easy," Ben bragged.

"You think so?" Penny seemed interested.

"I know so," Ben said. "I was going with this twenty-nine-year-old woman, and I had her popping off like a machine gun."

"I bet you never even had a piece of ass," Penny said. "But I'm ready to call your bluff." She stood up, unsnapped her jeans, took them down and off, and peeled her bikini pants off a lovely pair of legs.

Ben stared in disbelief. Here was a twenty-two-year-old college girl taking her pants off for him to screw her! And she was real knockout too! Nice, almost flat belly, neat triangular bush, and she had stripped down for him to fuck her! Ben let his own pants drop, revealing a steadily growing hard-on.

"Not bad," the girl said, looking down at Ben's dick with interest. "Not bad at all."

He pulled his undershorts off, went over to the girl, put his arms around her and kissed her. Her tongue went immediately into his mouth, and he meshed tongues with her, smelling her clean, sweet scent. His naked thighs touched hers, and their bellies were pressed together. His hard 'prick was shoved tightly against the girl's coarse-haired beaver.

Ben put his hand under her sleeveless top and found a bare boob. He felt her up, while he kissed her.

"Want to fuck me?" she whispered in his ear.

"I'm going to," Ben said and ran his hands over her bare ass. It was firm and nicely rounded, a lovely college-girl kind of ass. Ben went for her cunt. It was small and neat, very wet, and smelled sweet but raunchy. Ben guided her over to the couch, pushed her backwards until she was lying on it. He had no trouble getting her legs apart. She spread for him, and examined her cunt, and then slowly stuck his prick into her.

She was a hot one all right. As soon as she felt dick, she went sort of crazy, out of control, and started to fuck him. The temperature inside of her cunt was hot, Ben felt, and he ground his hips down on hers as he gave her his full eight-and-a-half inches of meat.

He fucked her well and expertly, and after a couple of minutes, she screamed and came, hugging him, and calling him her lover. Ben kept fucking her, feeling her ass, cupping both her cheeks so that he could push her naked hips against himself while he rammed his meat into her. She smelled so good and felt so good on his prick that Ben forgot about all the other girls and women he had fucked or wanted to fuck. He just wanted to fuck Penny, and he was doing that, and she came again, screeching and clawing his back. Ben kissed her and felt her up and kept right on fucking her until she popped off again.

"My god," she smiled up at him, tears in her eyes. "I'm never letting you go, young man. Can you come up here and give it to me like this every night?"

"I'll give you as much fucking as you want and as you need," Ben promised.

"You're so young," Penny said, "I mean, and you can keep it up so long."

"I can get it up again real fast after I come," Ben boasted. "I mean with a girl like you it isn't difficult. You're the hottest, the sexiest girl I've ever met."

He kept right on fucking her, while she put her legs up around his neck and crossed her ankles at his nape. He could get way up inside of her that way, and he did and she started to cry out with joy as she came again.

Ben brought her to another climax with powerful strokes that rattled her teeth. This tune, he waited until she shrieked out, then he flooded her womb with his hot spunk, pumping spurt after spurt into the screaming girl.

"Listen," Penny said afterwards as she played with his balls to get him ready for another fuck. "Promise one thing."

"Anything," Ben said, his prick getting hard again in the college girl's caressing hand. "Don't jack yourself off, Ben. I want you to save every drop for me."

"That's a promise," Ben said, and pushed the college girl onto her back. "I just hope you can take all that I can give you." He spread her cunt open and inserted his cock into her warm, wet cunt canal.

"I can take whatever you got," Penny said and began to return his fuck thrusts. "Just don't stop. Don't ever stop."

Ben thought that if there were a heaven, he must be in it. He popped his nuts off just as Penny came again. His prick barely went down. He kept on fucking the sexy college girl until he was rock-hard again. When she came off, he spurted spunk into her again. He filled her full of his juice as she went into her ecstasy.

He was still fucking her, carrying her into the kitchen five minutes later, holding her up by the ass-cheeks while she straddled him and rode his prick. He could fuck her while he cooked, while he ate, and while he slept.

Ben added water to the stew, covered it again, and laid Penny out on the kitchen table. Then he got on top of her, put his prick back into her willing cunt and fucked her to another screaming climax. He gave her three more before he shot his own nuts off again. He was still fucking her when the stew was done, and Penny begged him to stop so they could eat.

The End

More Books
From this Author

Seduced ~ All in me
Tied and Bound ~ Face in her friend's muff
Room Service ~ What happens in Vegas, stays in Vegas
Nancy ~ The skeleton behind her closet
Jesse's Pumpum ~ One hell of an aunt

**Happy readings!

Lightning Source UK Ltd.
Milton Keynes UK
UKHW020631130120
356857UK00011B/985/P